A Twist In The Tale

A JOURNEY INTO IMAGINATION

EDITED BY DEBBIE KILLINGWORTH

First published in Great Britain in 2023 by:

Young Writers
Remus House
Coltsfoot Drive
Peterborough
PE2 9BF
Telephone: 01733 890066
Website: www.youngwriters.co.uk

Printed and bound in the UK by BookPrintingUK
Website: www.bookprintinguk.com
YB0537S

Foreword

Welcome, Reader!

For our latest competition A Twist in the Tale, we challenged primary school students to write a story in just 100 words that will surprise the reader. They could add a twist to an existing tale, show us a new perspective or simply write an original story.

The authors in this anthology have given us some creative new perspectives on tales we thought we knew, and written stories that are sure to surprise! The result is a thrilling and absorbing collection of stories written in a variety of styles, and it's a testament to the creativity of these young authors. Be prepared for shock endings, unusual characters and amazing creativity!

Here at Young Writers it's our aim to inspire the next generation and instill in them a love of creative writing, and what better way than to see their work in print? The imagination and skill within these pages are proof that we might just be achieving that aim! Congratulations to each of these fantastic authors.

Contents

Emmley Gittens (11)	67
Poppy Dearman (11)	68
Mia De Angelis (10)	69

Gayhurst School, Gerrards Cross

Amelia Davies (10)	70
Emma Evers (10)	71
Ella Ceh (8)	72
Olivia Davies (10)	73
Amaya Shah (9)	74
Prianna Mann (8)	75
George Hawkins (11)	76
Emily Duong (9)	77
Ruby Adams (9)	78
Milan Joshi (8)	79
Aarav Shah (9)	80
Amar Atwal (9)	81
George Reeves (9)	82
Nefeli Malevitis (10)	83
Josh Singh (10)	84
Benjamin Taylor (10)	85
Sanjana Arun (10)	86
Savaan Patel (9)	87
Misha Peera (9)	88
Charles Maher (9)	89
Zachy Misan (9)	90
Carter Line (9)	91
Jacob Westbrook (9)	92
Matthew Singleton (10)	93
Alicia Wheeler (10)	94
Cameron Mochan (9)	95

Harris Primary Academy Haling Park, Croydon

Ishaani Shah (10)	96
Liam Browne (11)	97
Sadanah Mohammad Qureshi (10)	98
Fabian Jugariu (8)	99
Laura Mineva (8)	100
Aryan Kapoor (7)	101
Rosalie Williams (7)	102
Elisha Mendez (10)	103
Caiden Gordon (9)	104

Tayla-Rae Carter (11)	105
Christine F (10)	106
Matteo Douglas-Noble (8)	107
Aasiyah Coburn (9)	108
Francesca Tate (9)	109
Valerie Moreno (10)	110
Patrick Joseph (6)	111
Milania Blake (9)	112
Ali Abbas Virji (8)	113
Edwyn Rhys-Davies (8)	114
Aarushi Athavan (5)	115
Millie Moreno (9)	116
Leo McFarlane-Walton (9)	117
Alessia Skana (9)	118
Mary Zhang (10)	119
Zara Malik (10)	120
Elijah Hamilton-William (10)	121
Poppy Clarke (11)	122
Mateo Alfaras Gallego (6)	123
Yash Beeharry (9)	124
Amani Da Silva (7)	125
Patrick Smaranda (7)	126
Nataliya Singh (11)	127
Herb Anderson (7)	128
Umar Ahmed (5)	129
Zoha Khan (5)	130
Nabil Elnaggar (10)	131
Ruchika Tippisetty (8)	132
Amari Lee Williams-Bradnock (6)	133
Eliana Martinez Gooding (9)	134
Rohail Jamshaid (9)	135
Eva Tran (7)	136
Sohaib Qureshi (10)	137
Devansh Kayal (8)	138
Mira Navaneeth (6)	139
Mohamed Ali (9)	140
Mariah Barnes-Welch (10)	141
Harshini Karthick (10)	142
Neryah James (10)	143
Ruby Croucher (8)	144
Jodie Crawford-Ackim (10)	145
Adem Bayir (10)	146
Poppy Cope (10)	147
Idris Quddus (9)	148
Ethan Thomas Wilhelm (10)	149
Brooke Millen (9)	150

Ruzena Gupta (11)	151
Aditi Gunasekaran (8)	152
Elyse Rameswari (9)	153
Mia-Skye Ferguson (9)	154
Amirah Jallow (6)	155
Alexa Gardner (9)	156
Jacob Galarza (10)	157
Henry Croucher (10)	158
Cameron Crowhurst (11)	159
Malaak Imessaoudene (10)	160
Lottie June Hodge (11)	161
Harris Raja (9)	162
Lyra Rhys-Davies (5)	163
Naveah Ramnarace (6)	164
Oluwatomisin Oguntola (10)	165
Aaliyah Chan (9)	166
Aliyah Sayfoo (5)	167
Rayne Wilson-Watson (6)	168
Raphael Brazier (10)	169
Tianna Kelly (9)	170
Ryan Rahman (9)	171
Advika Yadav (6)	172

St Peter's CE Middle School, Old Windsor

Lucy Anderson (9)	173
Elizabeth Hunt (9)	174
Harriet Bannan (10)	175
Jessica Hyde (10)	176
Sophia McEntee (9)	177
Ava Jarmola (10)	178
Lily McBride (9)	179
Ilona Shevchuk (9)	180
Noah Richards (10)	181
Tara Khabra (11)	182
Harry Kirk (10)	183
Abigail Cleaton (9)	184
Beau Russell (10)	185
Hayden Davy (10)	186
Freddie Blackman (9)	187

MAX AND THE GLOWING STONE

"Bye, Mum."

"Argh! What is this? Some stone-like thing. What... it's glowing, I need to tell everyone at school."

"Guys, I saw a weird glowing stone, it looked magical."

"Haha!" exclaimed Bobby.

"It's not funny," shouted Max.

"Sorry about that," said Brad.

"Follow me," said Max.

Brad reluctantly agreed. After school Brad said, "Where are we going?"

Max said, "Watch."

"Wow!" exclaimed Brad. "How did you do that?"

"Don't worry," said Max in a calming yet respectful manner.

"Anyways I have to go."

"Bye."

"Bye."

"Mum!" said Max. "I need to tell you something..."

Ayub N'diaye (10)
Al Mizan School, London

THE LOST KITTEN

The sun shone brightly as Halima strolled through the park, the leaves crunching under her feet. She was waiting for Chloe when she noticed something... Instantly, she darted towards the sound. Creeping gently to see what it was. Halima was excited to find a tiny, cute kitten, softly purring. It was frightened. Delicately, Halima lifted the kitten to take it home. "Do you know anyone who lost a kitten?" Halima asked Chloe on the phone.
"Yes! Me!" Chloe replied excitedly.
She took a big sigh of relief and was extremely proud that she was able to help her friend, Chloe.

Jannah Hussain (7)
Al Mizan School, London

MECHANIC X

Late, in the village of Guahi, the muki spirit entered Mechanic X while he was sleeping. But little did the village know that there was an even bigger threat that was going to happen to the jungle of Parigal. When the sun rose the people of Guahi were starting to realise that Mechanic X was acting very strangely. He started to break down trees and yet even worse, killed the leaders of the pack (the king and queen).

In the distance, the village saw that Mechanic X was starting to tear down the rainforest which was his own childhood home...

Sakeenah Sikdar Mansur (10)
Al Mizan School, London

THE MONSTER IN THE WOODS

There was a boy named Jack. He loved going to his local woods so he could play. He went to the woods one day and he saw something moving. He suddenly saw a big monster. They both said, "Argh!" But Jack knew he wasn't that scary but he thought he was a bad guy. Eventually, Jack and Pete became friends. Jack and Pete had to sneak into Jack's house. Jack always sneaked Pete into his house. He gave Pete clothes and makeup to disguise himself. Jack's parents never knew and they lived happily...
But it was all a dream.

Naba Ahmed (11)
Al Mizan School, London

STORM AND THE TALES OF THE BEASTS

One foggy morning, Storm woke up. To his surprise he wasn't at his house, he was on a deserted island. A few feet away, he saw a mysterious blade stuck in a giant rock. A few seconds later he found himself walking and ran up the rock. He heaved himself up and saw a person dead with a cat. He immediately named it Whisper and heaved the mysterious sword out of the rock. He found himself with immense power. He then found himself with Zen, the lowest-ranked monster ever. He was shivering with fear until he remembered, it was time...

Yusuf Khan (11)
Al Mizan School, London

THE BETRAYAL

Zahra, Rahma and their team were the best superheroes of all time. But one day, Zahra and Rahma's team betrayed them and went to their enemy's side. They tried to get them back but it wouldn't work. A few weeks later they got into a fight. Zahra and Rahma didn't want to hurt their old team. Instead, they convinced them to join their team again but they said no. They tried to shoot Zahra and Rahma with an arrow but they ducked and it hit their team instead.
I woke up and realised it was all just a dream.

Zahra Bint Kayum (10)
Al Mizan School, London

MIGHTY STONE

"Dark Night, wake up!" we need to try to get the stone and fight the light," said Ghost Boy. "Okay," said Dark Night.

Dark Night had no choice but to get up and search for the stone. He bought out seven stones at a time and threw them at the light. Kong Hu the master of light set a plan, so late that night before starting he and his army exploded the sky with dark smoke. Ghost Boy ran but failed. Dark Night blasted the rock and hit the stone. Kevin ran and stole the stone and they won it.

Iftikhar Ahmed (10)
Al Mizan School, London

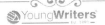

ZOMBIE LAND

One day in Japan, there was a man called Dave. He was a survivalist who fought zombies. An experiment went wrong in a hospital. There were zombies everywhere. Dave ran away from the zombies until he reached a big tower. He went inside and it was safe. Dave began living in the tower. He planted crops, made armour and guns, and he made a balcony to snipe zombies from far away.

Later, he saw a large zombie in the distance. He began shooting it but it was immune, so he built a wall to protect his base.

Safwan Motahir (11)

Al Mizan School, London

THE BATTLE OF ENCHANTMENT

A malicious monster had been reincarnated into an even more powerful and vicious monster... Zeradile. The vicious man who killed the monster before it was reincarnated was Zoceraz, a warrior known to all humankind. He trapped the beast in the immortal lake but it managed to come out and came after him. After, the god of war heard about it. He immediately charged in at the beast alone and he sadly passed. As soon as Zoceraz heard he was furious. He took his sword and slaughtered the beast with no mercy.

Khaaq Ishaaq
Al Mizan School, London

DEATH AND KILLER

Someone knocked on my door. As I walked to the noise, every step I took, my heart pounded faster and faster... I arrived in a quiet motion and peeked out of the window. There were police outside my house. It felt good knowing that, so, without any problems, I opened the door but it was a man. I asked him what the matter was. He replied, "I would like to do something that will make a big difference to your life..."

Without me having to answer he swung his baton at me and knocked me out.

Tawhid Mahmud (11)
Al Mizan School, London

SPACE MUSK

Elon Musk wanted to go to Mars so he hired his high-tech engineers to make a rocket that would go to Mars. He boarded the rocket and took off. He saw all the planets and even all the universes. But he went to another universe of his own, a different alien universe. He saw aliens, clouds and even planets which looked mesmerising. Soon he left the alien universe and went to Mars. Suddenly his rocket exploded and he was stuck on Mars. But would he be able to get back to Earth?

Muadz Al-Nizami (10)
Al Mizan School, London

THE BOY WHO GOT BETRAYED

I woke up on Saturday morning and went downstairs to eat breakfast. I noticed someone knocking on the door so I got up and went to the door to open it. I saw my friend there so I went outside to see what he wanted. He said he wanted me to go with him so I went to his house. I noticed it looked different to when I was there last. I saw a chair there. He asked me to sit on it. I did as he said and then he put some chains on me... "Argh!"

Ali Ahmed (10)
Al Mizan School, London

THE DRAGON'S CAVE

One day Mike went into a forest trying to find a big spider. Instead, he found himself in a mysterious cave. Suddenly from behind him, he heard giant steps and to his surprise, a giant dragon appeared. Mike was so scared that he was paralysed. The dragon tried breathing fire but Mike suddenly found a legendary sword and slayed the dragon.

Mohhamed Nomah Ali (10)
Al Mizan School, London

THE RUMOURS OF EMILY AND EVA

"Mum, can you retell the story of Emily and Eva?" asked the youngest.

"Fine, once more... There were two girls heading to a forest. Something happened with the trees, there were screams but no one came out."

"Ooh, was it on the news?" asked the oldest.

"No!"

"I've heard a rumour," said the middle.

"Tell us!" the youngest said.

"...Emily and Eva were in town. All of a sudden, a homeless person grabbed them. They were never seen again."

"That was amazing. It sounds so true."

"Fascinating."

"That's not true."

"Mum, isn't your name Emily?"

Mum replied, "I am Emily."

Isla-Mae Loveridge (11)

Ann Edwards CE Primary School, South Cerney

THE SECRET DUNGEON

Once upon a time, there was a girl called Isla. She was in her fun, amazing school. When it happened... Two people came holding bags full of gold. "What are you doing?" said their old teacher, Mr Chris.

"We need Isla," said the bigger one.

"Yes," said the smaller one.

"What will you give me?" said Mr Chris.

"This money," said the bigger one.

Isla was taken. They took her far away. Just then the bigger one scratched his head and Isla could just get away. She ran back but fell down, down, down and then she saw a door...

Harry Daffern (7)
Ann Edwards CE Primary School, South Cerney

THE DREAM WORLD

Once, there was a young girl with a big imagination but her life was upsetting. So one night she thought up a plan. She would dream her way to happiness so she slept and whilst she slept she dreamed and that dream brought her to a world of dreams. "I'm in a forest and that's a boy..." said the girl in a scared tone.

"My name's Emmi and you look like you need help."

"I do, I can't escape a bad dream."

"Well let's do this."

So off they went. Suddenly the boy said, "There's my bad dream..."

Hattie Young (9)

Ann Edwards CE Primary School, South Cerney

GINGER RUNS AWAY

Once upon a time, Gran baked a lovely gingerbread man. Gran said, "Grandpa go and get the kids."
"Okay," said Grandpa and Gran turned around. The gingerbread man ran outside and said, "I'm a small gingerbread man but you can't catch me." Connie and Matt chased Ginger until they ran out of breath. Gran and Grandpa chased Ginger through the town until Ginger stopped. He stared at other gingerbread men and ran into the gingerbread man shop. He looked around at the other gingerbread and then he grew bigger and bigger. Oh no!

Sienna Turner (8)
Ann Edwards CE Primary School, South Cerney

AUSTRALIAN AIRPORT GETS INVADED

Joey came to the biggest Australian airport. Joey was going to America with his step mum and dad. It was the busiest airport. There were cafes, shops, and restaurants but Joey's favourite store was the candy store. Just before he went in somebody grabbed him by the shoulder. "Stop!" said Joey. The robber replied, "No!"

Joey tried to grab his arm to escape. He did. The robber rushed as fast as he could. Joey saw his gate and rushed there. The robber saw him as he went in. Joey found the place and got the disguised robber arrested.

Luke Cranfield (8)

Ann Edwards CE Primary School, South Cerney

THE GRANNY AND THE KID

Once upon a time, there was a granny and a kid. The granny's name was Rose and the kid was Daisy. "Hey Daisy," said the granny.
"Yes?" said Daisy.
"Do you want to go to the pet shop?"
"Yes," said Daisy.
"Why do you want to get a dog?"
"Because it is fluffy and it is fun to play with as well."
"Okay, do you want another pet?"
"Yes," said Daisy.
So she bought the dog and the other pet for Christmas. She got a lot of amazing things. Wow!

Isla Leon (7)
Ann Edwards CE Primary School, South Cerney

SNOW FROM ANOTHER DIMENSION

Ava woke up one winter's day and rushed to look out of the window. It was snowing and the snow made her garden look like a crisp carpet. The trees looked like ice sculptures dancing in the winter breeze. Without hesitation, she rushed outside still in her pyjamas. As she stepped onto the crisp snow with no imprints, she could hear the muffled crunch underfoot. Out of the corner of her eye, she saw something rather strange, it was an ice sculpture. Not a tree but an igloo. Apprehensive, she strode towards it and entered a magnificently different world.

May Jewhurst-Baines (10)

Ann Edwards CE Primary School, South Cerney

THE PRESENCE

The girl felt a presence behind her, she peered over her shoulder. There she saw a tall man in a long black cloak and a hat covering his pale face. He whispered something and disappeared. The girl was stunned, flabbergasted. She started to sprint. She took a look behind her. In the distance, she saw a tall black figure. She turned her head back and ran faster. As Luna stopped to take a breath she heard a whisper, it was faint but Luna made out some words... "You... will... disappear..." Luna recognised the voice very clearly...

Imogen Mueller (11)
Ann Edwards CE Primary School, South Cerney

THE BROKEN PROPHECY

I was in an abandoned hotel. The paint was peeling off walls, and cobwebs filled every corner. I walked the halls searching for my friend. Dust rose every step I took then I heard a screech coming from a room where the door was ajar. I peered inside to see a horrifying sight... Suddenly, I awoke. Cold sweat dripped down my face. Then I heard the same screech from within my dream. I noticed a dark shadow in the corner of my room. I closed my eyes and when I reopened them the thing had moved closer... Everything went black.

Lily Hopkins (10)
Ann Edwards CE Primary School, South Cerney

BUNNY SAVES THE DAY

On a sunny and bright Wednesday, I was at a primary school in South Cerney. There was a supervillain battling a good guy, who was me. The supervillain was trying to kidnap the headteacher. I went to help and wrap the supervillain in toilet paper. Surprisingly, a bunny appeared and hopped in-between us. The bunny was so cute that the supervillain fainted. I called the police and they arrested the supervillain immediately. I walked away with the cutest bunny in the world. I called him Floppy and I took him home with me.

George Russell (7)
Ann Edwards CE Primary School, South Cerney

LITTLE RED RIDING HOOD

One day Little Red Riding Hood went out and saw a house. She knocked at the door but nobody was there. She did something nasty, she opened the door but the house didn't belong to her. She went inside and saw some porridge. She ate all of it and she didn't care that it was someone else's house Then she saw a chair and she was jealous because the chair was pretty. She didn't want to be jealous so she broke the chair on purpose and then she also saw a bed. The bed was uncomfortable so she went home.

Evelyn Thapa (6)
Ann Edwards CE Primary School, South Cerney

HUDSON AND THE BOOK

Hudson was sleeping in a normal house, on a normal street. Suddenly, he heard a colossal rumble. He woke. In the blink of an eye, Hudson saw a book snapping at the end of his bed. The book started to snap harder at him. The next thing he knew everything was pitch-black. Hudson opened his eyes and stared. Above him were bright blue eyes and a beaming smile. The sun reflected off his golden crown. It was a prince. Hudson picked himself up. A gigantic roar came from a wonky castle. Hudson and the prince ran...

Ollie Taylor (9)

Ann Edwards CE Primary School, South Cerney

THE BULLY AND THE CHILD

It was a sunny day. The child's name was Max. Max was walking at a lake. The lake was named Bow-Wow. Max saw an adult. He looked mean. He walked to Max and picked Max up. Max yelled, "Help!" Nobody helped and the bully chucked Max into the lake. Max found an exit from his world to the future. He was scared. Max was older than everybody else he saw. He was excited but everything was different. Max went to the shop to get sweets. The sweets were fizzy. Max got lots and lots. He had a sugar rush!

Blaze Sampson (8)
Ann Edwards CE Primary School, South Cerney

JACK AND THE GIANT

Once there was a boy called Jack who lived with his mother. They were very poor. So Jack's mother said, "We have to sell our cow, it's the only way." So Jack took the cow to the market. On the way, Jack met a strange man who gave Jack some magic beans and a beanstalk grew. Jack climbed it and found a giant. The giant let him in and gave him some money and food and sent him home. His mother was really happy. So happy that she gave Jack a really good dinner and they went to the shops.

Maddie Vivian (6)
Ann Edwards CE Primary School, South Cerney

MAGIC VIOLET

Once upon a time, there lived a girl called Violet and a boy called Jack. They were best friends. They played until the day came when they found out what school they would be in. They were scared so they sat down and hoped for the best... As Violet was going to get her answer someone kidnapped her. When she woke up she was in a dungeon. She accidentally shook herself and she had blue dust coming out of her hands. She was magic. Then, *boom!* She teleported back home. This story remains a mystery.

Phoebe Hopkins (8)
Ann Edwards CE Primary School, South Cerney

THE SPECIAL GIFT

Once upon a time, there was a girl, her name was Ebba. She was a horse rider and a Prime Minister but nobody knew. She lived in London. One day somebody came to see her. She was so excited because she was a professional horse rider. She was the same age as her and from then they were best friends.

A couple of years later some people came to see her. They came to see her because she was popular as a horse rider. When they found out that she was the Prime Minister they loved her even more.

Ebba Danhieux (8)
Ann Edwards CE Primary School, South Cerney

A WEIRD TIME

Once upon a time, there was a girl called Maddie. Maddie had a pet dog called Luna. One day Maddie had a sleepover at her friend Alfie's house. Maddie took Luna. The day went quickly. It was time for bed. All of them were asleep when a flying pig took them into a dream. They went up, down, left and right. Then they found a magnificent, shiny and beautiful gem. It was so shiny that it nearly blinded Alfie. They took it! Then a maze rose around them. They tried to escape but couldn't...

Ava Beckford (8)

Ann Edwards CE Primary School, South Cerney

THE ENCHANTED GIRL

One night a girl called Phoebe went to bed and decided to read a story. Phoebe started. She had decided on an old story and read out loud. Things started to disappear. Word after disappeared until everything was gone then Phoebe disappeared. Phoebe appeared at the start of a maze. She was worried. She started walking along the path. She looked around. She ran and ran and bumped into a wall. There were two doorknobs. Both doors were red, both doors had padlocks on. Phoebe was stuck.

Ella Johnson (9)
Ann Edwards CE Primary School, South Cerney

THE CHILD TEACHER

Once upon a time, there was a child who was a teacher and his name was Charlie. He was twelve when he started teaching but this class was different because Charlie teaches teachers! But Charlie was a strict teacher. When one of the adult students was naughty he would whack them on the bottom really hard. But then all the adults charged at Charlie and broke his neck. He had to go to hospital but when he recovered he realised that he had been rude so when he got back he became nicer.

Bella Hanks (9)
Ann Edwards CE Primary School, South Cerney

LITTLE RED RIDING HOOD AND THE WOLF

One day Little Red Riding Hood was scared in the forest, she was walking to Grandma's. She knew that the wolf was there. She got there at the same time as the wolf. "Grandma, I have nowhere to live I'm cold and I have no food, let me come in."
"I will help you feel better with medicine," said the wolf.
So they went in and gave Grandma medicine. Grandma said, "Thank you wolf," then Grandma felt better so he went.

Lewis Rennie (6)
Ann Edwards CE Primary School, South Cerney

LITTLE RED AND THE WOLF

One day Little Red Riding Hood was walking down the street when suddenly a wolf jumped up at her. Little Red Riding Hood ran as fast as she could, she was running to her grandma's. As soon as she got to her grandma's her grandma turned around but it was the wolf!

She ran back home but the wolf was still there so she ran around the house. The wolf was still there so she went to the shop and the wolf was still there so she ran back home again!

Esmae Clapton (6)

Ann Edwards CE Primary School, South Cerney

CINDERELLA

One day Cinderella was, as usual, sweeping the ground. All her life she had thought that her stepsisters were mean and she thought that because they made her do all the chores every day. She did not like that. But one day she found out that her sisters weren't mean at all when they let her go to the ball and dance with the prince. They danced all night until it was morning and the very next day they planned an amazing, fantastic, super good wedding.

Emily Widmann (6)
Ann Edwards CE Primary School, South Cerney

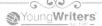

LITTLE RED RIDING HOOD

Once upon a time, a girl called Little Red Riding Hood asked her mum if she could give her grandma her medicine. She said yes so she ran to her grandma's house. It was in the woods. It was scary but Little Red Riding Hood was not scared. Suddenly she saw smoke coming out of a house. It was scary but she went in. It was dark. She started to look around the room for a switch to turn the light on. Then she could see in the house. She saw Grandma...

Harley Sollis (7)
Ann Edwards CE Primary School, South Cerney

MYSTERIOUS TEMPLE

A boy called Josh found a mysterious temple. He walked up to the temple and went in. He was walking anxiously but suddenly he walked into a trap and ended up in a maze. He tried to find an exit but he couldn't find it and a monster appeared. Josh ran for his life. There were two doors but Josh picked the wrong door which led him to a zombie apocalypse! He got a weapon but he had bad aim. Luckily the others were good at aiming so they survived.

Pranab Thapa Magar (8)
Ann Edwards CE Primary School, South Cerney

THE TALE OF MR AND MRS TWIT

Once upon a time, in an old house, there lived Mrs Twit and Mr Twit. One day some birds came but the birds were bad and one day the birds wanted to prank them. The monkeys helped by getting super glue that could stick them forever so they did it so then they started to paint the floor white like the roof and the roof like the floor then when they finished the birds put the glue down and Mrs Twit and Mr Twit stood on their heads and stuck forever.

Storm Sampson (6)
Ann Edwards CE Primary School, South Cerney

RED RIDING HOOD

Once upon a time, Red Riding Hood was going to her grandma's house but she didn't know that her grandma was ill and when she got to her grandma's house her grandma shut the door. When Red Riding Hood got in the house she gave her Grandma some medicine that made her sick but luckily Red Riding Hood could read the label and gave her Grandma some other medicine that made her well. Then Red Riding Hood and her Grandma were friends again.

Nathan McKenzie (6)
Ann Edwards CE Primary School, South Cerney

A MYSTERIOUS DREAM

Once upon a time, there was a girl with her sister in their bedroom getting ready for bed. They said to their mum, "We are going to bed."

Their mum said, "Okay."

They went upstairs quietly to their bedroom and said goodnight to each other. Then they went to sleep... Unfortunately, Devon and Freya both had a nightmare and they tried to wake up but they couldn't...

Who knows what would happen next?

Devon Anderson (8)

Ann Edwards CE Primary School, South Cerney

THE SNOWMAN AND THE PIG

Once upon a time, there was a pig who lived on his own and he built a snowman who came alive. The next day the pig looked out of his window and the snowman wasn't there so the pig ran into the garden and he could not believe his eyes. The snowman was actually gone so he went to look for him. The pig found the snowman and the pig took him back home. The snowman and the pig played together. The pig and the snowman lived happily.

Harriet Taylor (7)
Ann Edwards CE Primary School, South Cerney

YoungWriters

FOOTBALL LEGEND: MARCUS RASHFORD

At Old Trafford, there was once an amazing footballer called Marcus Rashford but the manager was a child. He trained them worse and worse every day but that didn't matter to Marcus he was still incredible. Suddenly the transfer window opened up. Marcus and his best friend, Bruno Fernandes, got teleported. They ended up at Barcelona. They won loads of cups in La Liga, seven Champions League cups and three UEFA League cups.

Charlie Lewis (8)
Ann Edwards CE Primary School, South Cerney

A BOY CALLED BOBBY

Once upon a time, there was a boy called Bobby. He lived in a castle. One guard got scared. He jumped out of the window and landed in a lake. The next day Bobby noticed another guard go missing. The next day, he went for a walk and something caught his eye. It was a gate he'd never seen before. As he walked in a creature came to him and said, "Go away!" He jumped out of the window and ran to the castle.

Archie Holmes (8)
Ann Edwards CE Primary School, South Cerney

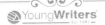

THE THREE LITTLE PIGS AND THE FRIENDLY WOLF

One day the three little pigs lived in their houses and the wolf went for a jog and he accidentally blew two of their houses down. He was so sorry that he helped the pigs to build their houses again. Not the one that was made of bricks though because he didn't blow that one down, it was too strong. They were best friends forever and ever and on Saturdays and Sundays, he went over and they played together.

Max Neale (6)
Ann Edwards CE Primary School, South Cerney

RED RIDING HOOD

One day Red Riding Hood went to play in the park. Then she went home to eat some cake, the cake tasted like vanilla sweets. When she ate the cake she loved it so she ate lots of cake. She went to have a walk around the forest. When she went around the forest something scared her. It was a wolf! The wolf ate her. The wolf went in Grandma's door but Grandma wasn't in her home so the wolf stopped.

Hannah Martin (6)

Ann Edwards CE Primary School, South Cerney

GOPAL'S FAMILY ADVENTURES

Hi I am Gopal. I live in a jungle with my family. We all had fun but one day the fun was over. It all started on a sunny day when I was going for a walk. I fell in a deep dark hole. And in the hole was a baby. Sorry, but it was not just any baby, it was my baby that I was trying to find in the first place. So I took the baby and tried to get out of the hole. I could not get out... *Ssss!*

Jessie Buchalik (8)
Ann Edwards CE Primary School, South Cerney

A STRANGE DAY AT SCHOOL

One day I turned up at school late. Normally the teacher tells me off for it but today it was the opposite. She was dancing! The children were laughing. I did not see that, right? The headteacher was playing with toys and somehow Mr Mobie was doing the splits! Mrs Collins was doing backhand springs and Archie was jumping off a building. Why was Albert pretending to be an angel?...

Noah Unstead (9)
Ann Edwards CE Primary School, South Cerney

THE CRAZY HEADTEACHER

Once upon a time, there was a headteacher. He was very nice and one day it was strange but somehow the headteacher was mad. He was dancing on the table! Seriously, like why? This was odd. The next morning he was happy, why? Because he'd won a dancing competition. Then he was playing golf in the cloakroom. I never knew he was doing this. He was also seen lifting a car...

Rory Foulkes (8)
Ann Edwards CE Primary School, South Cerney

RED RIDING HOOD

Once upon a time, there lived a little girl called Red Riding Hood. She lived in the woods and her mum told her to take some food to her grandma who was poorly. She was walking to her house and she did not want to get eaten by a wolf. As she was walking she saw a wolf so she ran to the house. When she got there she gave her the food and she said thank you.

Freddie Edlington (6)
Ann Edwards CE Primary School, South Cerney

JADON SANCHO: THE BEST FOOTBALLER IN THE WORLD

At Old Trafford, there was an amazing footballer called Sancho. He was taller than the others because they were children. They were still good at football but not as good as him. The manager was very happy. This season they won the league again. They always got to the finals and won. It was amazing!

Hudson Perring (8)
Ann Edwards CE Primary School, South Cerney

RED RIDING HOOD

One day Little Red Riding Hood was on a walk and she was so happy to see her grandma that she jumped with excitement. There was a fox. She was going to eat Grandma. Red Riding Hood was so upset she knocked down the bed then the fox ran off. She was so happy then she went to sleep.

Amelia Spence (7)
Ann Edwards CE Primary School, South Cerney

LITTLE RED RIDING HOOD

One day Red Riding Hood was looking for her grandma's cottage in the forest. When she got there her grandma was hiding from a wolf in the cupboard and the wolf was pretending to be Grandma. Little Red Riding Hood fell over in the forest because the wolf was chasing her.

Lily Libbreck (6)
Ann Edwards CE Primary School, South Cerney

NAUGHTY LITTLE RED RIDING HOOD

One day Red Riding Hood woke and went downstairs. Her mum said, "You need to go to your grandma's house."
But instead of going to her grandma's house, she went into the woods. And in the woods, she found a wolf that said hello in a kind voice.

Scarlett Sweet (6)

Ann Edwards CE Primary School, South Cerney

LITTLE RED RIDING HOOD

One day Little Riding Hood's mum let Little Riding Hood give Grandma medicine and so she went. But when she got to Grandma's house there was a wolf inside. Her grandma was fed the medicine and Little Red Riding Hood was shocked when she saw the wolf.

Harry Dinh (6)
Ann Edwards CE Primary School, South Cerney

THE BLACK HOLE

Once upon a time, there lived a zookeeper called Sky. She worked at a zoo with two animals... A sloth and a tiger. One day Steve and Gopal jumped into a black hole and teleported into a scary town. Steve and Gopal called for help so loud but it was silent.

Izzy Newton (8)

Ann Edwards CE Primary School, South Cerney

THE BETRAYAL

Once, on a normal day, two friends decided to go on a walk but soon they realised it was not all it seemed. "Where are we?" said Tom.

"I'm not sure," said Jack.

But as Tom turned around Jack was gone. "J-Jack, where are you?" but no one answered.

Tom decided to sit down and wait but that was a bad idea. The bushes started rustling and as he looked around Jack was standing there. "You're so pathetic why would you trust me?"

"What?"

"You know I come from a line of suspicious parents!"

"No!" Tom said. "Well, goodnight."

Seren Elston (10)
Buckingham Park CE Primary School, Buckingham Park

THE LAST

"£2.40," said the cashier. I handed over my £5 note. She rummaged through the till for £2.60. As she passed me the change she asked where my dad was. He works 24 hours a day so I never see him.

"Put your hands up!" shouted three masked beings as they stormed through the door.

Screams emerged out of everyone's mouths, including mine. I knew this was my last day. Last breath. Last everything. The cashier's hand quaked as she gave them the money. As they swiftly moved out the shop, the leader revealed their identity... "Dad?"

Kai Grainger (11)
Buckingham Park CE Primary School, Buckingham Park

THE KNOCK

Knock, knock, knock...
He had finally arrived. I ran to the door, grabbed the handle and swung the door open. "Hi!" I said with a smile. The figure stormed into the house. "A hello would be nice," I said kindly.
The man stayed silent. He looked back at me. His eyes had a stern look. He had a black cape and wore grey leather boots. He turned back and rummaged in the drawer. "Who are you and can you go?"
The man pulled out a safe. "Finally!" the man said. "Oh, it was a dream, thank God!" I sighed.

Yashriya Thushyanthan (10)
Buckingham Park CE Primary School, Buckingham Park

THE UNEXPECTED

Me and my brother saw it... Santa's sleigh. We bolted and leapt in. Santa was delivering presents so we were alone. My mum was at work for the night. Oh no! Santa was in with us. We were freezing. We were above the clouds. I tapped Santa. "Argh!" he screamed. He lost control of the sleigh. The reindeer were gone.
"Oh no! No! No!" I said.

The sleigh broke down. Santa didn't say a word. We were both speechless. We found the reindeer, they were rolling along the ground. They were dead. I ruined Christmas. No more presents for children.

Charlie Butcher (10)
Buckingham Park CE Primary School, Buckingham Park

THE GOBLIN ON THE LOOSE

I skipped down the road, opened the gate and froze to the spot. There was the goblin. "Boo!"
"Who are you? A garden goblin?"
"I have made us tea, come and join me."
I stepped forward and the goblin jumped down off the fence. Quickly he slammed the door shut. I was locked out. His evil laugh grew louder and louder. What was I to do? *999* I thought, I called, I explained. They came, smashing glass and the police were in. All I could hear was, "Catch me if you can!" His face revealed the policeman.

Amelia Slatter (10)
Buckingham Park CE Primary School, Buckingham Park

BEWARE THE BARYONYX

Lava dripped through the ceiling of the Ingen compound. The ground shook. A red light flashed in a tunnel, illuminating a bipedal shape with a crocodile-like head. I screamed in terror. My colleague, Claire Dearing, staggered backwards. The baryonyx roared. "P-pass me t-the chair," Claire said. "Pass me the chair!"

I threw it over to her and she put it under the extendable ladder so she could reach it. She climbed up it, reaching for the exit hatch. I followed her. The baryonyx roared, the ladder extended. I screamed in terror...

Shakil Gordon (10)
Buckingham Park CE Primary School, Buckingham Park

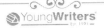

THE SCHOOL TRIP

Eleanor set her stuff up inside the tent next to Lara's tent. Soon enough it was night and everyone gathered around the campfire. Everyone except for Lara. Eleanor noticed this and told the teacher. Lara was missing. At midnight Eleanor heard an ear-piercing scream. Everyone heard it. Soon enough we found her encased in a slimy creature. Eleanor ran for Lara but was met with darkness. Eleanor woke with a gasp in her comfortable bed. She sighed. It was just a dream. She turned on the TV only to be met with Lara's face listed as 'missing'.

Evie Mills-Hodgson (10)
Buckingham Park CE Primary School, Buckingham Park

SCHOOL TRIP

Thud! I slipped on the icy floor as I got on the minibus. When everyone was seated our teacher started driving. After a few minutes, we knew something was wrong. The smell of rotten eggs filled the room. It had been an hour and I knew it shouldn't take this long to get to the zoo. *Thump!* Jake dropped to the floor. The driver was smiling. But he wasn't our teacher. He was... he... I couldn't breathe. I was feeling more and more light-headed. The last thing I remembered was a man smiling at me as I passed out slowly.

Hrithika Sadineni (10)
Buckingham Park CE Primary School, Buckingham Park

NOT-SO-MERRY CHRISTMAS

My mum and dad said they would get me a ginger cat for Christmas. But there was just one problem. My dad had not returned since 6am! He was gone for 9 hours. I was so worried until I heard a bang. I also heard my loving father screaming in the garden. Oh no! In the shadows I saw a pitch-black figure that looked just like a woman, she had a gun in her hand. I shivered with fear. I knew this was my last day. The lady yelled, "Take that you brainless man!" Wait, that was my mother!

Sahithiya Ajantharuban (11)
Buckingham Park CE Primary School, Buckingham Park

THE CRASH

Crash! The car in front of me had crashed but when I looked in front the car didn't have a single scratch. The person who owned the car dropped dead. I ran away. I couldn't get caught again after what I'd done. On my way home I saw police cars. I ran as fast as I could. The police chased after me. They knew I killed the chief. I ran down the alleyway. I knew they couldn't get me there but when I got to the end he was there. It was the chief...

Gurnoor Dhesi (10)
Buckingham Park CE Primary School, Buckingham Park

THE BLACK TRAPDOOR

I was being dragged onto the rough sandpaper-like floor. It was hot and I could not see anything as there was a blindfold covering my eyes. *Clunk!* A door opened. I saw a man dressed in an ebony shade of black. He was holding a gun. My life flashed before my eyes. He shot. *Pow!* He shot again. *Pow!* I turned behind me to see what he was shooting. It was millions of zombies. I shrieked. He took off his mask. Who was this man? It was my dad!

Logan Macuha (10)
Buckingham Park CE Primary School, Buckingham Park

MISSING

I jumped on the bus and we headed to London. We all had a really good time until there was danger. We stopped off to eat something. I was so hungry. I was ordering my food when suddenly it went black. Someone grabbed me. Everyone saw and tried to help, but it was too late. I was in the bus, they took me. I was scared. She went back and got someone else, it was my friend, Rose. She hopped on her seat and started driving. We were a great pair, mother and daughter!

Emmley Gittens (11)
Buckingham Park CE Primary School, Buckingham Park

BETRAYED

Crash! I slammed the door open and walked inside. The headmaster wasn't at his desk like usual, he was on the floor, murdered. I bent down and touched the wound. Suddenly the police burst into the room. "There! She has blood on her hands! Arrest her!" the chief shouted. They grabbed my arms and dragged me out of the building.

As I was getting taken out I saw my best friend standing with a grin on her face. She was the killer.

Poppy Dearman (11)

Buckingham Park CE Primary School, Buckingham Park

A DREAM

One night I was asleep when there was a rising clatter. I jumped out of bed and slowly tiptoed downstairs. I had to push the door open because of the amount of snow there was. But what I saw was like a dream. There was a chocolate river and giant candy canes everywhere. It was like a wonderland! I went to try some of the chocolate and it was the best thing I had ever tried. Then I awoke. It was a dream, or maybe, just maybe, it was real...

Mia De Angelis (10)

Buckingham Park CE Primary School, Buckingham Park

PORKY'S DEMISE

Huffing and puffing Fluffy blew. With no success, she began to whine. Sadly, she flopped down in exhaustion. Inside the little rustic cottage Bill, the eldest porker, confidently reassured his terrified younger brothers that all three were safe and secure. "Let us be friends with this dangerous creature!" suggested Roastabon. Later, "Hello, what is your name?" asked Bill hesitantly.
Finally Fluffy replied. In no time, all four became best of friends. Sadly, days later, Porky passed away from pigilitus. Wind howling, creatures silent, trees swaying in sadness, as Countrylane Town mourned.
Later, Fluffy vanished into thin air. The dark woods?

Amelia Davies (10)
Gayhurst School, Gerrards Cross

THE WEDDING

Cinderella was getting ready for her wedding. Before she got changed, Cinderella decided to check everything was ready for the wedding. On her way down she knocked on Chance's door. When nobody responded, Cinderella pushed open the door and gasped at what she saw. Chance was kissing Rapunzel! "What!" Cinderella gasped, heartbroken. "How could you?" Her sorrow turned into rage. Cinderella burst into tears and ran from the room. The one person she thought she could depend on for anything had betrayed her. She ran into the forest and found a witch, who gave her a potion for her heartbreak.

Emma Evers (10)
Gayhurst School, Gerrards Cross

THE ANIMAL CIRCUS

It was Saturday morning; the animals were getting ready for the afternoon circus performance. Lepall and Katey, the leopard trapeze artists, were checking their ropes. Morris the monkey was looking for his helmet, Zachary the fire-performing lion was greasing his fur and Bob the bunny was unpacking his magic tricks. The circus filled with people and the performances were exciting the crowd. Bob was finishing his act when Morris' cannon misfired and he was launched towards the flaming hoops. Bob waved his wand, Morris froze in midair, then floated gently to the ground. Morris was saved, the crowd erupted.

Ella Ceh (8)
Gayhurst School, Gerrards Cross

THE FOREST

Silence. There was nothing to be heard except my own heavy breathing. The glistening moon shone majestically down through a thick lattice of soft tender leaves as blotches of sparkling stars were glimpsed through the canopy of ancient treetops. Tall slender firs reached up like shooting spears into the sky. Like a stealthy jaguar ambushing his prey, I carefully crept through shadowed trees searching desperately for a visible trail weaving through the undergrowth. I was lost. Suddenly, demon-like figures began to approach from the shadows, a hand sharply landed on my shoulder. I let out a muffled scream...

Olivia Davies (10)
Gayhurst School, Gerrards Cross

THE STEPSISTERS' COMEBACK

Dear Diary,

Cindy's so mean! Ever since her daddy died she's been saying we're revolting and useless and she's been treating us like slaves - but we've had enough! Lately, we've turned the tables around and now she's doing *our* dirty work. We're telling her to do the laundry, wash the dishes and even clip our toenails!

You can't blame us, there are only a few more days till the ball! Mother has picked out our dresses and Cindy's doing our hair and makeup. It's the least Cindy can do as she's not going to the ball - or so we thought...

Amaya Shah (9)

Gayhurst School, Gerrards Cross

THE ALLEYWAY

Aaron walked through the twisted, uninhabited alleyway. It was wedged discreetly between dilapidated buildings. There were walls eaten by weather and time. He knew someone was watching him. He felt it. Aaron's pulse began to quicken, he felt uneasy by the threat of the encompassing darkness. Suddenly there was an ominous lightning strike, shark-white against the inky-black sky. He heard a vehicle behind him. He ran choked with fear but he wasn't fast enough. He was pulled into this van. A man said in a deep voice, "We're from the year 3000, we need you to help us..."

Prianna Mann (8)
Gayhurst School, Gerrards Cross

THE COUNTDOWN TO BLOODSHED

Hercules stood in a barren wasteland with his comrades waiting to ambush his enemies. While brandishing his sword, he scanned the battlefield looking for any areas of weakness. Hercules and his trusted warriors readied themselves for the brutal battle. The opposing legions had been stalking one another for days and this was to be the crescendo. He rallied his troops and sprinted towards the enemy, hoping to intimidate them with his war cry. As they did so, there was a familiarity to the reverberation of sound. Each army paused, realising that it was in fact their own long-lost battalion.

George Hawkins (11)
Gayhurst School, Gerrards Cross

THE SUSPICIONS

In Laston Town, there lived a clever boy called Ted. His family lived at number 4 Pinewood Drive. Ted and his mum and dad felt suspicious about their neighbours at house number 5. The stone path approaching their house was covered in blood. Their house was beautiful on the outside though. Once, Dad received a letter saying: 'Come to our fantastic house'. It was from their neighbour, Captain Rogust. A dash of nervousness went through Ted. Ted rapidly sprinted to the nearest window. He gazed at Rogust's creepy house. All of a sudden, their massive house turned into a sausage!

Emily Duong (9)
Gayhurst School, Gerrards Cross

SCIENCE CATASTROPHE

One day a boy called Mason was walking to science class in his brand-new Nike Airs. His favourite lesson was science. The teacher, Dr Jaxon, loved experiments with chemicals. When Mason got to his seat he noticed Dr Jaxon was acting a little weird. Two school bullies had put purple chemicals in his drinking bottle. Suddenly he turned into a zombie! Mason was terrified, so he quickly made an anti-zombie potion using his knowledge of the periodic table. He quickly poured it over Dr Jaxon's head and hoped that it would turn him back to normal. Fingers crossed...

Ruby Adams (9)
Gayhurst School, Gerrards Cross

METALFIST THE BRAVE

Once upon a time, there was a boy named Metalfist. He was drawing and suddenly a huge, fierce monster raged towards him and dropped a huge detonating bomb. Luckily, it didn't hit him. Metalfist started to concoct a plan to escape from the monster. Next to him was a cascading waterfall. Metalfist took a gulp of water, he was parched. The monster strode towards him and Metalfist spat the water at him. He was drenched. Metalfist shuddered at his victory. He shook his fist at the retreating monster then suddenly his hand brushed against his duvet. It was a dream!

Milan Joshi (8)
Gayhurst School, Gerrards Cross

THE WANDERING SEA MONSTER

"Watch out!" They saw something. A dark shadow swam across the sea. It looked like a snake except bigger. It jumped up from the sea, bumped the ship and then went back down. Everyone started screaming and running to evacuate. The captain, Adam, tried to calm things down but that didn't work.

The monster crashed into the ship again. It began to sink. People screamed and shouted. They ran to find life jackets and the mini boats. When they were all in the sea, Adam said, "Stop!" because the monster was a robot and he was controlling it!

Aarav Shah (9)
Gayhurst School, Gerrards Cross

THE RESTAURANT BOOKING

One sunny summer morning Tom Walski woke up and jumped out of bed. Tom was fifteen. When he went downstairs, his mum came rushing to him and exclaimed, "Have you booked your dad's birthday surprise yet?"

Tom quickly rushed to his room and called up a fancy restaurant. The restaurant's phone number was 065798 so he called and booked a table. Later that day Tom told all his relatives the address. They arrived there later the next day but it wasn't a fancy restaurant, it was a swimming pool. Tom realised he had called the wrong number.

Amar Atwal (9)
Gayhurst School, Gerrards Cross

THE SEA MYSTERY

One hot day, Alex was at the beach relaxing in the sun's calming heat. Suddenly he noticed a shadow coming toward him. A man screeched, on a phone... "Police! There is a shark in the water. Please help me!" Alex saw droplets of tears running like cheetahs down his cheek. He had to solve this sea mystery! Alex slithered down the beach cautious about what would happen. His heart pounded uncontrollably. He saw the shark! In a flash, he jumped into the water. What he found was truly curious... It was a man swimming. Now that was very, very odd!

George Reeves (9)
Gayhurst School, Gerrards Cross

STRANGE SCHOOL SCENARIO

Yet another day at school but this day was different. Schoolgirl, Harriet, was going on a school trip. When she arrived she quickly hopped on the bus and the journey started. It started with normal things like the teacher getting the kids to sing songs but suddenly the bus jolted and then stopped. The driver did not know what happened and said that they were not out of petrol. Then a shadow cast around the bus and everyone disappeared. Except for Harriet. She looked around the empty bus and searched for help but there was no one to be seen...

Nefeli Malevitis (10)
Gayhurst School, Gerrards Cross

THE WICKED WOLF

In the dismal darkness, a lone wolf howled dreadfully with an ear-splitting cry of pain. Even though the wail was as loud as a trumpet nothing could illuminate the wolf in the darkness, not even the dark red glow of rage in its eyes. As the wolf embraced for its final howl the world went silent. It seemed as if everything was dead. Nothing stirred. In the vicinity, there was a fierce rustle in a nearby bush. Again, silence. It was like time occasionally took breaks and paused. Just then, the howls turned into growls and thuds were heard...

Josh Singh (10)
Gayhurst School, Gerrards Cross

A PORTAL

I was walking through a dimly lit corridor. The passageway seemed to be never-ending. My bright torch flashed and left me in total darkness. Suddenly, I rounded a bend and a light blinded me, shining with all its might. What could it be? Magic? A secret power? A portal... I reached forwards, still shielding my poor eyes. As soon as I touched the shining globe, I was dazed. The swirling, white mist; the soft feeling of the ground, and the groaning of a... man? Suddenly I woke up. It was dark and freezing. Trees loomed over me. Where was I?

Benjamin Taylor (10)
Gayhurst School, Gerrards Cross

LOST IN THE WOODS

Lilly and Ava were assigned to pick apples. They had to make sure they were soft and delicious. None of them matched their expectation so they decided to go into the woods. At least Lilly did. Ava was hesitant at first but once again she had to follow her best friend. They had found the apples but couldn't find their way back. Lilly was pretty but not that bright. Ava started panicking, Lilly told her to calm down. They advanced deeper into the woods. They were in the Mystique, a forbidden area. They turned around to find a light...

Sanjana Arun (10)
Gayhurst School, Gerrards Cross

PERCY JACKSON

Percy is a boy who lives in the underworld and aimed to destroy Olympus. He had finally freed his father, Hermes, from Tartarus. He was now building an army of monsters including the Minotaur. Before he could destroy Olympus he had to destroy Camp Half-Blood. He travelled through the underworld and the sea of monsters. He finally arrived at Camp Halfblood. Percy threatened the camp with all his monsters. There was a battle, a battle of heroes and monsters. Olympus was his, Camp-Blood would be destroyed. The titan lord would rise again.

Savaan Patel (9)

Gayhurst School, Gerrards Cross

THE UNKNOWN WORLD

One cold morning Lana went to a forest to get wood for her mum. Lana realised that there was a portal in front of her. She jumped into the portal. On the other side of the portal, she couldn't believe her eyes. There in front of her stood a half-wolf, half-human. It was eating hungrily. Her whole body felt numb. She was shaking with fear. The half-wolf and half-human didn't realise she was there. This was her chance... She quickly jumped back into the portal and was panting. She began trembling while she walked home.

Misha Peera (9)
Gayhurst School, Gerrards Cross

POINTLESS PETER AND THE BORING CHORES

At home, Happy Henry and Pointless Peter were in the living room. Peter was getting annoyed with baby programmes so Pointless Peter shoved Henry out of the chair. He watched his own horror film. Henry was scared and shouted, "Mum!"
Peter got in trouble and was sent to his room.
Mum called, "Peter!" Peter didn't come down.
"Peter, it's time to do your chores!"
Henry came but Peter didn't. So Happy Henry did all of Peter's chores and got all the pocket money!

Charles Maher (9)
Gayhurst School, Gerrards Cross

THE EVIL SNOWMAN

One day in the forest there was a snowman. This snowman wasn't normal like other snowmen. This was an evil snowman. There were lots of children in the park. The snowman was trying to kill the children. But there was a chase, a super long chase, it went on for such a long time. The children were running for ages. They were running through puddles and bushes. But eventually, the chase ended and the sun came out and the snowman melted. The children were so relieved and hoped this would never happen again.

Zachy Misan (9)
Gayhurst School, Gerrards Cross

THE FRIENDLY DRAGON

Many moons ago, there lived a young boy named Carter (age 12), and he was an adventurer. His next quest was to defeat the dragon guarding the gold. He set off. He found the cave where the dragon lived. He stepped in and pulled out his sword. The dragon didn't growl, he whimpered. He put his sword down and got closer and closer and the dragon exclaimed, "Take some gold!" and Carter did. The dragon smiled at him.
In the end, Carter did not want to kill him but it was his quest so he did!

Carter Line (9)
Gayhurst School, Gerrards Cross

LIAM AND THE ALIEN

One night Liam was driving back from work and listening to Radio 5 Live. Then suddenly a huge meteor shot out of the sky, still blazing hot from the Earth's atmosphere. Suddenly there was a massive explosion and Liam's car shot up 50 feet in the air. Luckily Liam's jumper acted like a parachute so he jumped and only got a few scratches. When he landed he saw an alien pop out of the rock. Liam was frightened but when he saw the alien it smiled at him, so he edged closer until he had a friend.

Jacob Westbrook (9)
Gayhurst School, Gerrards Cross

THE DREAM

I darted through trees and bushes whilst branches whipped me like I was their slave. I reluctantly peered back and regretted it. The ground as I knew it was disintegrating and about to consume me with it. I jumped back into life. I started to run but the second I picked up speed the roots threw me to the ground. My whole body was in agony so it was then, at that point in time, my instincts told me to give up so I did and I lay there and fell into the void.

Then I awoke. Alive. A dream!

Matthew Singleton (10)

Gayhurst School, Gerrards Cross

NO WOLVES HERE

One day there was a grandma who lived in a little cottage. A scary wolf, who wanted to eat her, knocked on the door. She took one look at him and was so angry that she ate the wolf instead!
After eating him poor Grandma felt sick but just then her lovely granddaughter, Little Lucy Lime, arrived with some flowers for a visit and nursed her back to health. From that one day, no wolf ever came to the door again. So the next time you see a wolf who tries to eat you, you know what to do.

Alicia Wheeler (10)
Gayhurst School, Gerrards Cross

THE WANTED WARDEN SPY GUY

The evil warden was very pleased with himself for locking up every hero in town but the guards recognised the warden. The guards opened the prison cells and all the heroes made a team to find the evil warden. But the evil warden was always surrounded by guards so it was hard to get him. The heroes saw a big group of guards and the evil warden was behind them. The heroes used their superpowers to defeat the guards and knocked the evil warden out cold and locked him in prison forever.

Cameron Mochan (9)
Gayhurst School, Gerrards Cross

MYTHICAL MYSTERY

Victoria stumbled upstairs, dragging her feet behind her. It had been a long day's work... Cleaning oil from the cotton mills, picking up fabric that had fallen from the machines and adjusting the 'contraption' that worked the mill. It was only after several hours of the continuous, tiring bore that Victoria received consent to get into her uncomfortable, pine bed that had yet been awaiting her. She hastily rushed into bed as the overseer switched the lights off and strode out of the room. Victoria's eye caught a shadow scuttling across the dormitory. What was the mystical creature?

Ishaani Shah (10)

Harris Primary Academy Haling Park, Croydon

THE CABIN

In the middle of a creepy forest, was an abandoned cabin. A young boy named Alexander heard about the cabin, so he ventured through the forest to find it. behind it, were two ginormous trees. After examining the trees, he noticed a portal leading towards an unknown world. As he entered the portal, he discovered mythical creatures such as goblins, trolls, fairies and dragons. Alexander started to explore the mysterious world but suddenly the portal doors began to fade away. He rushed towards the portal but a troll stopped him. With an evil laugh, he shrieked, "You're never going home!"

Liam Browne (11)
Harris Primary Academy Haling Park, Croydon

A HORRIBLE SCHOOL TRIP

The rain was pounding relentlessly. We were almost there. "Sorry, we'll have to stop at Camp Buntrees... there's nothin' we can do," screeched Ms Hawkins, her voice like nails on a chalkboard. After this announcement, sighs of despair were flowing through the sweltering bus. What had fate cooked up for us now? All of us were assigned cabins, mine was 13. My friend, Alice, was in cabin 12. Soon after, I went to visit her. While walking, I could hear some people laughing; others crying. After hearing tears, I slowly ambled back into cabin 13... Blood! It was everywhere...

Sadanah Mohammad Qureshi (10)
Harris Primary Academy Haling Park, Croydon

THE WONDERLAND OF FREEDOM

Simon and Lucy went on an adventure to the woods. "Wow!" Lucy saw an old, abandoned castle. They decided to explore it.

The guard seemed friendly and had heavy iron armour. Suddenly, the door slammed loudly behind them. They found themselves locked in a cold, dark tower. After a night spent there, Simon saw a shiny button. They both pressed it. The wall opened up to something that looked like paradise. On a huge, wooden board it said: 'The Wonderland of Freedom'. It was full of twinkly gems. "Looks like we are free to go onto bigger, better adventures!"

Fabian Jugariu (8)

Harris Primary Academy Haling Park, Croydon

THE STORY OF THE SUPERHERO'S DOG

Once, in a pet shop, Cracker spotted a superhero looking straight at her. Suddenly, her friends were trying to tell her something and she thought they were excited, but she was wrong. When she got there she was in a supervillain's lair! Cracker was so panicked and knew why her friends were so strange. She saw that there was a waterfall nearby and that gave her an idea. Surprisingly, her friends came along. Pom-Pom spotted a figure. The others pushed the supervillain down the waterfall. Pom-Pom called Cracker. Cracker went to the figure and pushed it down the waterfall happily.

Laura Mineva (8)
Harris Primary Academy Haling Park, Croydon

ENGLAND VS BRAZIL

It was the FIFA 2022 World Cup and England were playing against Brazil in Qatar. It was an extremely hot and blazing day but a thunderstorm was brewing. The England team were training for their match which was taking place the next day. Suddenly the thunder and lightning began and a lightning bolt struck the training ground. An expression of shock appeared on the England players' faces so they hurried back to their hotel. The England players woke up to discover they were now children. The team was ready for their match. Who do you think won... England or Brazil?

Aryan Kapoor (7)
Harris Primary Academy Haling Park, Croydon

MAGICAL FOREST

In the dark, gloomy forest, Rabbit saw an immensely beautiful gate. Sophie, Rabbit and Wolf went to check it out. It was covered in stardust and toadstools as big as mountains. There was a cold breeze and the smell of sweet flowers. Sophie was delighted. Wolf ran off and the others followed. Suddenly they found a waterfall. The shimmering water crashed onto the jagged, slippery rocks. They jumped into the magical water. When they got out they fell asleep. Sophie woke up and the magical forest had disappeared. It had all been a dream. No rabbit, wolf or magical forest.

Rosalie Williams (7)

Harris Primary Academy Haling Park, Croydon

EXTINCT ADVENTURES

Happily, two twins and two friends were going on a deadly adventure (the creators of Jurassic Park). They went on a coach that took them to Extinct Adventures. When they arrived the two twins and their friends went to put up tents. 24 hours later, they woke up and then started to explore. Later they then heard something say, "Evacuate now! There is a killer dinosaur!"

They couldn't evacuate so they made shelter. Then there was a dinosaur called Demon Slayer and they eventually killed it, or did they? Where were the bones of the body? Was it fake?

Elisha Mendez (10)
Harris Primary Academy Haling Park, Croydon

DANIEL, THE THREE-HEADED MONSTER

This story is about Daniel, the three-headed monster who lived in a hut on the riverbank. Children walking by the river always threw stones and eggs at Daniel's hut, upsetting him. Daniel used to be a really nice monster who just wanted lots of company. Daniel's family were from Croydon but Daniel lived in Greenwich. He moved away from his family because they treated him like the children outside. Daniel had had enough of them. He wanted to make an example of them by roaring outside. The kids stopped and ran away crying as Daniel showed his true colours.

Caiden Gordon (9)
Harris Primary Academy Haling Park, Croydon

BEACH DAY

A group of teenage friends went to the beach. They were eating ice cream and making jokes. Two of them decided to go for a swim in the sea. Accidentally, they swam further out than they intended. Next thing they knew, a massive wave was heading towards them. Frightened for their lives, they were screaming, "We're going to drown!" Their friends watched helplessly from the shore. All of a sudden, the wave slowed down as it reached them, surprisingly pushing them back to shore. They took a sigh of relief and lived to tell the tragic tale. What a day!

Tayla-Rae Carter (11)

Harris Primary Academy Haling Park, Croydon

THE MAGICAL SPELL

Once upon a time, there was a girl called Milly who was seven years old. She had a friend called Ava. Suddenly she heard a clamorous, loud, magical spell from outside the classroom. Everybody gasped when the teacher turned into a bird and then the spell turned her back. The excited, exuberant children looked at the teacher and said, "Miss, you turned into a bird!"
She said, "Where am I? I was still teaching!"
The spell promised not to come back ever again in class. They all had a celebration with fruit cake. They were very happy.

Christine F (10)
Harris Primary Academy Haling Park, Croydon

IT WAS JUST A DREAM

Charizard is the best and only superhero in New York City. Cruising in his black Bugatti, keeping the baddies and enemies away. Before Charizard knew it, his worst enemy, Mad Knight was in town and he'd come to pay Charizard a visit. *Slap! Bang! Wallop!* They fought to the death because only one superhero or one villain could rule New York City. Charizard was kind and caring and protected the people. The Mad Knight wanted to take over the world. He won. Charizard fell down, down, down. Suddenly he woke up. It was all a dream... *Boom!*

Matteo Douglas-Noble (8)
Harris Primary Academy Haling Park, Croydon

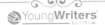

A LOT OF ROYAL LIES

Once, there lived a princess called Melody. Sadly, her mother went missing after her fourth birthday. She couldn't remember clearly, all she knew was that her mother was beautiful. One day Melody overheard her father talking about an underground prison. Curious, Melody went to the guards and they all said there was a prison! It was on the bottom floor. When she entered the prison she saw her mother. When she went over, someone grabbed her arm. It was her father! Then he pulled out a gun and shot his own daughter. Finally, they lived unhappily ever after.

Aasiyah Coburn (9)
Harris Primary Academy Haling Park, Croydon

DRIZELLA, THE STORY OF THE STEPSISTER

A long time ago, in a very old posh house, there lived a family. It was not a loving home. Drizella and her sister, Anastasia were very rude and mean to their stepsister, Cinderella. However, Drizella never felt good about this behaviour, but couldn't say no to her sister.

One day, she decided to do the right thing and say sorry to Cinderella. From then the girls were respectful towards each other. Anastasia didn't want to be left out, so she understood that she needed to change as well. This was the best decision. It was finally a loving home.

Francesca Tate (9)
Harris Primary Academy Haling Park, Croydon

THE OTHER WORLD

Many years ago there stood an ancient mansion that belonged to the McKenzies. There was a single daughter in the family, Lesley, who was always curious for miraculous adventures. She always thought that her house was full of secrets. A second later she noticed a square door in the wall. Curiously she reluctantly picked up her blade and started cutting it out the wall. She thought it was a deplorable thing to do but she wasn't going to let that stop her. She unlocked the door and suddenly a spiralled tunnel led the way... Similar to her dream yesterday.

Valerie Moreno (10)

Harris Primary Academy Haling Park, Croydon

PLANET EARTH

There are eight planets in the solar system. They are Mercury, Venus, Earth, Mars, Jupiter, Saturn, Uranus and Neptune. The planet we live on is called Earth. Earth is the third in distance from the sun and the fifth largest of the planets in diameter. Earth is not completely special. Earth has only one natural satellite, the moon. Earth is truly unique among the planets of the solar system. It is also very beautiful with white clouds, blue oceans and brown lands that shine against the black backdrop of our solar system. We should try and keep it that way.

Patrick Joseph (6)
Harris Primary Academy Haling Park, Croydon

THE CURSED BUS

One rainy day, Mia and her friends were on a school trip. But as soon as they turned there was a big bang... The bus stopped. Mia's friends were saying, "What's happening?"

The bus fell down a steep hill and the bus driver passed out as the kids screamed for help. Other buses passed but didn't hear... The others didn't survive.

After that, every single day she went to a different school when they were having a school trip. People were actually being traumatised because she wanted revenge. She was described as the Devil.

Milania Blake (9)
Harris Primary Academy Haling Park, Croydon

THE WORLD CUP FINAL 2022

The World Cup Final is here! In this final England play Argentina for the second time! England starts off and Rashford passes the ball to Harry Kane and Kane shoots. He scores. 1-0 to England. Now Messi has the ball. Di Maria shoots and scores! The English fans complain that it isn't a goal and the referee doesn't count the goal. Instead, England gave Messi the ball and finally the goal counts for Argentina but they still lose because Rashford, Kane, Saka and Sterling all get two goals! This means England are the champions for the next four years.

Ali Abbas Virji (8)

Harris Primary Academy Haling Park, Croydon

A NOT NORMAL DAY

One day, I went down to have breakfast. It was pancakes today. I guzzled them down like a wolf. I went back upstairs so I could get a game but instead of a cupboard, I saw a secret passage. It led me to a troll's bridge and he was reading. It was 'The Three Billy Goats Gruff'. He mumbled, "Those goats are so noisy!"

Quickly I chatted with the goats and told them, "You are so noisy!"

So the goats never annoyed the troll again. *The troll isn't the baddy, it's the goats*, I thought. I returned back.

Edwyn Rhys-Davies (8)
Harris Primary Academy Haling Park, Croydon

THREE LITTLE PIGS

Once upon a time, there were three little pigs. One pig built a straw house. Another pig built a stick house. Another pig built a brick house. The bad wolf huffed and puffed and blew the straw house down...

"Little pig, little pig, let me come in," the wolf said to the third pig. But the brick house was not blown away. The wolf said, "I am hungry."

The three little pigs gave him food. The wolf said, "Sorry," and, "thank you." They became friends. Then the wolf and the three little pigs played together.

Aarushi Athavan (5)

Harris Primary Academy Haling Park, Croydon

CAT IN THE FOREST

Coco went into a scary forest with her friends and she got her phone and made a video whilst walking around. After, her friends were scared but Coco was not and Jack told everyone to stop and go home.

Everyone else shouted, "Yes!"

But Coco exclaimed, "No! Let's stay here and explore the creepy forest!"

As they were walking through the creaking trees, they saw glowing ruby-red eyes watching them. Then Jack told everyone he saw red eyes except Coco because she was doing her video. Everyone else hated it there.

Millie Moreno (9)

Harris Primary Academy Haling Park, Croydon

THE SUPERHERO THAT IS AN EVIL VILLAIN

I'm a superhero fighting crime and working for the FBI. I go undercover and look like a normal citizen, people don't know I'm a superhero. The FBI give me awesome missions like finding out who stole the 1.3 billion diamonds but I already did that and it took me only four hours to find the person who stole the diamonds. Also, when I'm in superhero mode I fight bad guys like Doctor Evil, Hot Evil, Ice Freezer and more.

But what isn't known is I'm really an evil villain and there's a bomb going off in five hours...

Leo McFarlane-Walton (9)
Harris Primary Academy Haling Park, Croydon

THE KNIGHT AND THE MONSTERS

Once upon a time, there lived a great knight. His name was Robert. One early morning, he spotted a monster and fought it until he killed it. A few days later, you would think I'm lying... ten monsters reappeared. This was all happening in an enchanted forest. Believe it or not, it was the hottest day of the year. It was 60°C so the knight was hot and exhausted. He noticed the 10 scary monsters had reappeared. He fought immediately! He was the best knight in knighting history. So there you are, the story of the knight and the monster!

Alessia Skana (9)

Harris Primary Academy Haling Park, Croydon

IMAGINARY WORLD TO REAL WORLD

In an imaginary world there lived a young girl called Lucy. One day a special paper stopped in front of her. She didn't pay attention and signed to go in the portal. When she entered the portal her eyes popped and instead of candy trees there were real trees. After some time she wanted to return back to the imaginary world but she couldn't find a portal. She finally decided she would make one. After she made a portal and returned back everybody was surprised. The scientists weren't able to make one but Lucy was able to make one.

Mary Zhang (10)
Harris Primary Academy Haling Park, Croydon

THE TRIP THAT WENT SO WRONG

One day a group of kids went on a school trip to a desert island. The group were staying there for three days. Once they arrived they walked to camp, along the way a snake slithered from the trees. They all froze but their teacher ran away. After spending the night alone, they wanted to explore. After a few hours they reached a cave full of bright shiny blocks. "Gold!" the children screamed. They grabbed the gold and ran off. As they ran with the gold a black hole sucked them up. Since that day the children weren't seen again!

Zara Malik (10)

Harris Primary Academy Haling Park, Croydon

TIKO, THE BANANAS AND MONSTERS

I'm Tiko, everyone's favourite fishy. I'm going on a mission to become the best fish ever. I need to defeat every type of monster, but right now I'm battling a half-cat, half-mouse monster. Luckily that is the last monster in Atlantis. But now the Banana Army is trying to make a limited edition banana robot made of moon rock. I need to get to the moon with my Giga mecha fishy. By the time I get there, it's all been destroyed by the bananas, including the Nanamoon, and also Fishlantis (the nickname for Atlantis) is gone!

Elijah Hamilton-William (10)
Harris Primary Academy Haling Park, Croydon

NOISES

It was late at night, Lily could hear the sirens of the ambulance. She closed her eyes to fall back asleep. A deafening bang rippled down the street. She could hear the piercing cries of children and the devastating sighs. She peered out the window but nothing was there. She shut her eyes again. Only this time an immense shadow cast over her door and she heard the cries of her mother. She looked again and nothing was there. Suddenly, a dark figure leaned over her and their eyes hypnotised one another. She then realised it was all a dream.

Poppy Clarke (11)
Harris Primary Academy Haling Park, Croydon

THE THREE LITTLE HUNGRY MICE

Once upon a time, there were three little mice. They were very hungry because they couldn't find any cheese where they lived. So the three mice went to many houses but none of them had cheese. They were starved of cheese. They went to another street. The three little mice couldn't believe their eyes... They saw a market full of yummy cheese! The window was open so the three little mice climbed a ladder which was there. They jumped through the open window and they ate all the cheese they wanted. They ate it all and they were full.

Mateo Alfaras Gallego (6)
Harris Primary Academy Haling Park, Croydon

LITTLE RED RIDING HOOD WALKS IN THE WOODS

Little Red Riding Hood was told not to go through the forest, but she did! Whilst walking in the forest she saw some lovely flowers and she started picking them. She was tired so she sat under a tree. It was then that she noticed a shadow. She wanted to know what it was. It was moving towards her, a big scary bear! Little Red Riding Hood was frozen with fear. She wanted to run but couldn't move.

Then the bear said, "You better wake up or you'll be late."

She woke up and said, "Phew, it was a dream!"

Yash Beeharry (9)

Harris Primary Academy Haling Park, Croydon

THE THREE LITTLE PIGS

A long time ago, far far away, there lived three pigs. They stayed in a small village across a green field. Over the years, they collaborated as a team to build their own houses and they found it loads of fun. One day they came across what seemed to be a kind-hearted, grey-haired wolf that they'd never seen before. As they got to know each other they introduced themselves. Pig one was called Amani, pig two was called Justin, pig three was called Tais. The wolf was called Gihan. They got along very well. They liked to build together.

Amani Da Silva (7)
Harris Primary Academy Haling Park, Croydon

THE MYSTERY OF FLANNAN ISLE

A keeper that used to live there was now a ghost that was so, so evil that killed anybody that worked there in the lighthouse. Actually, the ghost was an old man who lived in a house next to the lighthouse. He was very, very angry because the light was not letting him sleep and he turned into a ghost. The entrance gate and door to the lighthouse were closed. Ducat and Marshall's oilskins and boots had gone missing. Whatever happened to the two lighthouse keepers on Flannan Isle sadly remains a mystery to their families to this day.

Patrick Smaranda (7)

Harris Primary Academy Haling Park, Croydon

THE HOUSE

'Twas a cold October night. The wind engulfed our small cottage on the hillside. Most of the tiles were shattered to pieces but our family of four still stayed there during the bone-chilling, freezing night. Papa was out cutting some wood for our fire tonight. He seemed to take quite a while. Eventually, he came home. However, me and Cecilia were already in bed. Cecilia and I peeped through the splintered door. Papa was cheering but Mama didn't seem to match his energy. He held this strange form. It said 'tree house'...

Nataliya Singh (11)
Harris Primary Academy Haling Park, Croydon

DISGUISED GRANDMA

Once upon a time, Little Red Riding Hood was walking through the woods when suddenly a wolf appeared. She ran as fast as she could then she met a friendly woodchopper. Little Red Riding Hood ran and ran then she finally got away. She kept walking along and then the wolf came back. Little Red Riding Hood just couldn't run anymore. The wolf then went again. She finally reached Grandma's house and opened the door. The wolf was in the house. But then the wolf talked! It didn't sound like a wolf. Grandma was disguised as a wolf!

Herb Anderson (7)

Harris Primary Academy Haling Park, Croydon

HANK AND HIS PET DOG

Hank woke up feeling very Hank! He got up and walked out of his bedroom. He approached the top of the mountain. Hank heard a loud growl and was very scared. A big scary monster appeared in front of him and whispered, "Help! I am lost." Hank decided to help the scary monster. They walked until Hank saw his bedroom. The monster ran into Hank's bedroom. The next morning when Hank woke up he saw his pet dog, Jeffey, next to him. As Jeffey walked away he was getting bigger and looking like the big monster he saw last night...

Umar Ahmed (5)

Harris Primary Academy Haling Park, Croydon

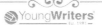

THE PRINCESS AND THE OLD LADY

Once, there was a little princess. She went to the forest to pick apples. In the forest, she saw a nice old woman. She said, "Can you pick up my bags? I have 1000 bags."

The princess said, "Of course I can."

But when she opened the bags they were full of stolen toys. The princess was shocked. The old lady was actually a witch and wanted to steal the princess' toys too. The princess ran as fast as she could and called the police. The police caught the witch and put her in jail. The princess was happy.

Zoha Khan (5)

Harris Primary Academy Haling Park, Croydon

CHUBO CHUBEECE'S DAY

Once upon a time, there was a lonely boy who lived in an orphanage. One day a man came and said, "Can I have that boy in the blue?" They agreed. He named him Chubo Chubeece who was a good boy and helped others. Later, a supervillain appeared and began destroying the world, but the father knew he had to stop him. He tried protecting Chubo, but soon found out that he was the supervillain. He had to continue what he began, but could he? Soon people thought Chubo had vanished, and they enjoyed the moment while they still could.

Nabil Elnaggar (10)

Harris Primary Academy Haling Park, Croydon

THE THREE LITTLE BEARS AND THE WOLF

The three little bears walked in the glacial wind. As they were hungry, they looked for some food. All of a sudden, there was an apple tree. They climbed up the tree to scavenge for food. They had a lovely time whilst they consumed their apples. Just as they thought it was perfect, a wolf appeared and a girl stood behind the wolf. In shock, they screamed as they thought it was dangerous. The younger bears were calm but the older bear wasn't. The bears had a plan to stop the wolf causing trouble. He was defeated. They were happy.

Ruchika Tippisetty (8)
Harris Primary Academy Haling Park, Croydon

THE THREE LITTLE PIGS

Once upon a time, there were three little pigs. They lived with their mummy in a stick hut. When their mummy was out shopping a big bad wolf knocked at the door and shouted, "Let me in!" then blew down their stick house. The scared pigs hid in the brick garden shed. The wolf fell asleep while trying to blow the shed down so the pigs made their escape but noticed the wolf was wearing their mummy's glasses and shoes. They realised it was their mummy stuck in a Halloween costume and she just wanted some help all along.

Amari Lee Williams-Bradnock (6)

Harris Primary Academy Haling Park, Croydon

LITTLE RED RIDING HOOD

Once, there was a very young girl called Red Riding Hood. She was told by her mother that there was a nice wolf in the forest whose grandma was sick and her mother wanted her to give the wolf's grandma some cookies. Here's the thing, she loved eating wolf but they were vegetarians, but she was so hungry she went to eat the wolf. They met when he was going to his grandma's house. Red Riding Hood followed the wolf. Next, she pretended to be the wolf's grandma. But then her mother came and grounded her for months.

Eliana Martinez Gooding (9)

Harris Primary Academy Haling Park, Croydon

THE THREE LITTLE WOLVES

We all know the three little pigs, right? Well, after I went away when I couldn't blow their house down, I saw something horrible. Right in front of my eyes, they got bigger. They grew claws and fur from nowhere, and I saw that they were wolves the whole time! I ran back home as fast as I could. A day later, the local newspaper came out. It said: 'Wolves on the rampage! Big bad wolves'... I saw they had been terrorising towns and houses. They would move away and go to the city. Well, guess I'm going to retire!

Rohail Jamshaid (9)
Harris Primary Academy Haling Park, Croydon

GREEN EGGS AND ORANGE HAM

Mr Purple was an ordinary man. He loved the colour purple so named himself Mr Purple. One day he heard his doorbell ring and saw a young boy called Thunder. Thunder said, "Try green eggs and orange ham."

Mr Purple looked at the meal in disbelief. This food was not purple so it would not be good. Thunder constantly followed Mr Purple saying, "Try it, try it!"

Eventually, Mr Purple gave up and said, "I will try it," and once Mr Purple tried it he said, "I am in love with this!"

Eva Tran (7)

Harris Primary Academy Haling Park, Croydon

SOHAIB'S BIRTHDAY TO THE FUNFAIR

Sohaib and his dad were going to the funfair because it was Sohaib's birthday. Sohaib was elated, excited and happy, he had never been to a funfair before. Sohaib ran as fast as he could to grab his things while his dad was in the car. Sohaib dashed over to the roller coaster to go on it with his dad. Suddenly the roller coaster started to fall in the mud. He was having an amalgamation of feelings, he'd never experienced anything like this before.

Sohaib disappeared into the Stone Age. No one ever saw him again.

Sohaib Qureshi (10)

Harris Primary Academy Haling Park, Croydon

TOM AND THE MAGIC DOOR

One day Tom was playing a game with Molly. Then, while Molly was playing on the slide, Tom noticed a purple door in the bushes. After Tom saw the door he wanted to go in, so he left Molly. When Tom opened the door he was shocked. He noticed his parents drinking water on their bed. Tom said, "You know there's everything I own in this secret place." He didn't care about his television and his couch floated in the sparkling sky. Not to mention his car. This was absolutely crazy for Tom to even see all of this.

Devansh Kayal (8)

Harris Primary Academy Haling Park, Croydon

THE MYSTERY

Once, there was a boy who always walked to school. When he was walking to school he saw a flying car before cars were even invented. So he sat in the flying car and it flew to a mysterious jungle. All the animals were hiding from winter because every November a perilous creature came out. Nobody could see him because he was fast. The boy found the creature, it stood right before his eyes. It was a massive starfish. It was scared and shrunk.

Just then my mum woke me up saying, "It's time for school, Mira."

Mira Navaneeth (6)

Harris Primary Academy Haling Park, Croydon

THE KING... WHO WAS NINE

King Edward was dying, but the heir was only a child! Earl Hans Godwinson would be crowned on the 9th December 2022. Hans was titled the youngest monarch in British history. He made his speech. "I, King Hans, will serve as your king." On the other side of Europe, King Luther loathed Hans. He despised him. He brewed a potion that would make Hans grow immensely. King Luther then sailed far west, and presented the potion to Hans in the form of hot chocolate. Hans couldn't resist, and that choice changed his life.

Mohamed Ali (9)

Harris Primary Academy Haling Park, Croydon

THE UNKNOWN

Ryllie woke up to a house with mould on the roof. When they opened the door to a mystical world they wanted to go back into the house but only saw a young boy who took their hand and ran into a land of flowers in an unknown direction. Ryllie ran after the boy and stopped at a cliff. Ryllie felt a shove and fell off the cliff. Ryllie opened their eyes and was met with a hug. "I thought you were dead, you idiot!" a voice cried.

"Who are you and where are we?" Ryllie asked, not remembering anything.

Mariah Barnes-Welch (10)
Harris Primary Academy Haling Park, Croydon

THE GREAT GOOD WOLF AND THE MAGICAL GLOBE

In a forbidden forest, a creature lived in a penniless cottage with a heart of kindness and wisdom. His name was the Great Good Wolf. He was a guardian of the forest for many years and controlled the magic globe of the forest. One day, a group of three pigs came and snuck into the wolf's house. As soon as they were caught, the wolf fought hard and imprisoned the pigs for stealing the globe from him. From then on, the globe remained safe in a place full of hope, love, patience, respect and dignity. The place was safe.

Harshini Karthick (10)

Harris Primary Academy Haling Park, Croydon

HIS NEWFOUND RESPECT

Onyx the cat was happily eating his food in the knowledge that his treasures were hidden away in his litter box. That was until he remembered what day it was... Change of litter day! Shocked and fearful, Onyx ran into the front room only to see that the malevolent Mr Plastic Bag was back again. But this time he would take away all of Onyx's things. He let out an agonising cry of despair and to his rescue Milo, his brother, swooped in and tore the bag to shreds. From that day on Onyx had a newfound respect for Milo.

Neryah James (10)
Harris Primary Academy Haling Park, Croydon

THE RAIN TOURNAMENT

Alex loved to do ballet, she had been practising for the Rain Dance Tournament since August. The tournament was only two weeks away. One Monday evening in November, as Alex and her mum were walking from dance practice the air turned suddenly colder and the ground was slippery underfoot. As Alex reached the zebra crossing she felt her tummy flick and she flipped into the air. She landed with a crash and instantly felt a flash of pain in her shoulder. Would she be okay for the tournament or would her dreams be shattered?

Ruby Croucher (8)
Harris Primary Academy Haling Park, Croydon

ABANDONED CABIN

In the forest lay a cabin. It had been in the woods for centuries but it still looked as if it had been recently built. Jade, a fourteen-year-old girl, had always passed the cabin. She always wondered why it had looked so brand new. On a Wednesday afternoon, she went to investigate. Jade pushed open the creaky door and her eyes quickly scanned the room. She noticed something move beneath a box so she moved it. There was a portal. Out of nowhere, she began to levitate but little did she know then, it was just a dream.

Jodie Crawford-Ackim (10)
Harris Primary Academy Haling Park, Croydon

DREAMS IN A DREAM

One day, a boy named Lester was wandering in a lavender field when suddenly a huge portal appeared and sucked him right in. He woke up in bed and noticed all the colours were inverted. He saw a strange shadow coming towards him and jumped right to Lester. He woke up again but this time, it was even weirder. He woke up in the ocean. A big mythical creature, a huge one, kept on splashing the waves against him. Lester randomly had a sword and swung it at the monster. He earned a mysterious item called the Phantom Award.

Adem Bayir (10)
Harris Primary Academy Haling Park, Croydon

THE BODY SWITCH

There lived a girl named Emily. She had a school day coming up. Emily went to a never-ending school and met her friend, Ella. All of a sudden, the bully, Alesha, came stomping over to them. The next night, the bully snuck into Emily's room and poured and potion onto her. The next morning, Emily went into the bathroom and looked in the shiny mirror. Emily called Ella and explained what had happened. Ella said she would fix it. The next day, Emily was her normal self again but she was now the bully and was mean.

Poppy Cope (10)

Harris Primary Academy Haling Park, Croydon

THE HALLOWEEN HORROR

It was nearly Halloween. Mike was on his way to school when he spotted a toyshop. He went inside to have a look. He found a cute teddy bear. He adored it. On Halloween, he took the teddy to trick or treat with him. Mike got so many sweets because of the bear's cuteness. While he was making his way home, he thought to himself, *what happens if I lose my baby doll-eyed bear?* When Mike tiptoed to bed he heard a horrifying noise. His bear turned into a monster! Without hesitation, he dashed out the door...

Idris Quddus (9)
Harris Primary Academy Haling Park, Croydon

HANSEL AND GRETEL

There were two siblings named Hansel and Gretel. They were kicked out of the house into a haunted forest. At the edge of the forest, they found three houses. One was a meat and potato house, the other was an appetiser and the final one was a sweet house. In each house, there was a witch and they were arguing about whose house was tastier. Hansel and Gretel waited until the witches left. They examined the houses before tucking into their three-course meal and when they finished they hid and watched the witches cry.

Ethan Thomas Wilhelm (10)
Harris Primary Academy Haling Park, Croydon

NOT EVERYONE IS DIFFERENT

Once, there was a beautiful lady called Casey. She moved into a new town. Casey loved to dance. One day a boy offered to take her dancing. Suddenly, Casey hated dancing. She was worried that if she liked things other people did she would not be unique. So she decided to give up all her dreams. Casey did that because other people do dancing and singing too! Not a few people do singing and dancing, a lot of people do it. She then went to the park. There were lots of people who also liked the park. She was equal!

Brooke Millen (9)

Harris Primary Academy Haling Park, Croydon

THE WITCH'S GRAVE

Me and my four other friends were playing catch with our lucky ball. Suddenly, Clara threw the ball so high, that it was out of my reach and it went soaring through the navy azure and landed in the most dreaded place of all... 'The witch's grave', or so it was known because the very name was enough to send shivers down a man's back. We had a quarrel over who was going to fetch the ball. Me and Clara were getting it. When we reached, a man spoke from behind. I realised there were two shadows...

Ruzena Gupta (11)
Harris Primary Academy Haling Park, Croydon

MYSTERY NEIGHBOUR

One sunny morning, I got out of bed and thought it was a normal day for me however I saw that my amazing neighbours were packing their things and leaving. I was devastated by this news. My mum told me that our new neighbours were moving in the next day. I was biting my nails in school and my mind wasn't been working. When I got home I started to research who could be my neighbour. Finally, I found out that my new neighbour is an FBI agent... This was absolutely unbelievable for me. I kept this a secret.

Aditi Gunasekaran (8)
Harris Primary Academy Haling Park, Croydon

THE DRAGON'S BAD DAY

One rainy day, there was a dragon called Michael and he was depressed. He got ill, so took medication. Suddenly he found out it was the wrong medicine, so it actually turned him into a human. The next day, he freaked out. They lived in a city with no humans, only dragons and aliens. The aliens found out so they helped him. Michael hated being a human, so he couldn't wait to go back to his normal self. It was Christmas the next day and he saw the nails of a dragon and thought he had got very, very lucky.

Elyse Rameswari (9)
Harris Primary Academy Haling Park, Croydon

SANTA'S NEW JOB

Santa was working in his shop. He was going to deliver to a farm so he did. He thought that it would be a normal boring day of delivering. When Santa went to the farm, he realised that a farmer's life might suit him better. He thought that being a farmer was the best thing that anyone could do. He had been wanting a new job for a while. When he applied all of the elves cheered. They started talking about who should be the next Santa. All of the elves argued. They all thought they should be Santa.

Mia-Skye Ferguson (9)
Harris Primary Academy Haling Park, Croydon

IT IS A BEACH LIFE

Once upon a time, Moana lived next to the beach. It was always summer where she lived. Moana lived in Hawaii, where the beaches were all beautiful and sandy. Moana loved to go to the beach and enjoyed spending lots of time there. One bright, lovely, sunny day, Moana was dancing in the waves and playing on the beach. She was making sandcastles and playing different types of ball games with her brother, sister, mother and father. They also took a boat to another beautiful, lovely island. It was all a dream.

Amirah Jallow (6)
Harris Primary Academy Haling Park, Croydon

LIGHT SHOW

Once at a normal camp, there was a captain who was evil. There was no running water nor fun activities only work. He hated all the kids. It was the end of summer. One day till it was time to leave. Suddenly, a monster made of light caged them. They stayed for hours. Then they remembered they had a mirror which set them free. They all knew who trapped them so they managed to get into his office. They made an explosion but there was no one there so they left and told their parents but they laughed.

Alexa Gardner (9)
Harris Primary Academy Haling Park, Croydon

THE EVIL LION

In a forest was a lion. The king of the jungle, he was the saviour of the trees and the animals, or so they said. Animals thought the lion was a god. Since he was the king of the jungle, he was a brave animal. However, only the lion knew that on the outside, he was a king but inside he was an evil villain that destroyed the last king. The regular lions knew about the last lion king because they were there when it happened. The regular lions were good to the animals but the king was even better.

Jacob Galarza (10)
Harris Primary Academy Haling Park, Croydon

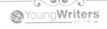

THE MYSTERY CUPBOARD

It was 3023. No one lived on the Earth except me. Most of the universe was left undiscovered. In this world, there was a mystery cupboard. No one had been brave enough to peek. I opened the door to an alarming creak. Inside there was a twinkling light. I stepped forward toward the light. I was greeted with faces from far and wide. My gut instinct was to hide. With a deep breath, I continued on hearing the sounds of a welcome song. The sight that greeted me was one I never want to see again...

Henry Croucher (10)
Harris Primary Academy Haling Park, Croydon

JONATHAN AND THE RETURN OF VOLDEMORT

Jonathan went on the new Hogwarts train. There were new sweets such as chocolate bats. When they arrived at Hogwarts they were sorted into their houses. Jonathan was selected to be in Gryffindor. In the morning, they learnt how to make objects levitate. They learnt which plants were good or bad, they also learnt the history of Hogwarts. After they had a lesson with Professor Black. In the afternoon they made objects disappear into thin air before going to their dormitories and talking.

Cameron Crowhurst (11)
Harris Primary Academy Haling Park, Croydon

THE THREE NAUGHTY PIGS

Once there lived a wolf who was extremely shy. He made a house of straw. Then, all of a sudden, three naughty, horrid pigs came. The initial one blew the straw house away, so the wolf built a stick one. Once again, it was blown away by the second pig. After, he made a house of bricks. The pigs had no luck. They tried to get through the chimney, but the wolf started a fire in it, so one by one they blasted out of the brick house. They passed their mum's house and reached the moon.

Malaak Imessaoudene (10)
Harris Primary Academy Haling Park, Croydon

BOY DOG

On Friday, after school, I went to go on a walk with my dog. This was my first time by myself. When I was at the park I noticed a strange eerie forest. I'd never seen it before, that was unusual. I decided to put my dog on a lead but I was too late. Dexter rushed off into the woods. I started running but he was gone. After a couple of minutes, a boy came by with chewing gum in his mouth. I said, "Have you seen my dog?"
He looked at me and said, "Woof!"

Lottie June Hodge (11)
Harris Primary Academy Haling Park, Croydon

THE THREE-HEADED BEAST

Once upon a time, a mythical beast came back to ancient Greece... The Hydra, a three-headed beast. The Greeks sent their best heroes. The heroes had no chance so they sent 50 warriors. The warriors found out that the beast was hiding in Sparta. Shocked, surprised and flabbergasted the warriors saw a vault of gold. The warriors asked, "How did you get so much gold from the Hydra?"
Then the Hydra gave gold to everyone. That is how Sparta became a successful empire.

Harris Raja (9)
Harris Primary Academy Haling Park, Croydon

SOMETHING CRAZY

Monster and Lola were best friends. They never spent time apart. But there was somebody who hated Lola and he was called James. James saw a pearl that said, 'Your secret sister is Lola!" He didn't believe the magic pearl. He decided to smash it! He ran and ran but he went into another world where the three little pigs ruled. They even ruled the wolf! He tackled the wolf then Monster and Lola came through the dimension. Then they all skipped home to get some snacks.

Lyra Rhys-Davies (5)

Harris Primary Academy Haling Park, Croydon

THE WOLF THAT DIDN'T BLOW

Once upon a time, there were three little pigs. Then a wolf came and said hello. The three little pigs built three houses, one was made out of straw, one was made out of sticks and one was made out of bricks. Then the three little pigs let the wolf come in each house. The three little pigs were not scared of the wolf because the wolf was friendly. The wolf did not blow the houses down. The three little pigs became friends with the wolf. And they all lived happily ever after.

Naveah Ramnarace (6)

Harris Primary Academy Haling Park, Croydon

THE OCEAN'S CAVE

Into slumber he goes... drifting through the water. He leaves the safety of the boat and eagerly swims to a colourful reef. Suddenly, he is taken away by a mighty current, leaving him stunned in a cave. When he wakes up, the water appears to be an iris colour. There is a peculiar smell of roses, although the cave is full of coral. Soon, a shoal of fish arrive. Their scales glisten in the shimmering liquid. But wait, this isn't true, it is just a dream. Thank goodness!

Oluwatomisin Oguntola (10)
Harris Primary Academy Haling Park, Croydon

THE GIRL THAT WAS THE HERO

One day a girl called Ivy went on a school trip up the hill. As she got ready to go to school she had a feeling in her gut, but she chose to ignore the feeling. She walked into school feeling happy but as she got on the bus her stomach started to do the biggest flip. She knew something would go wrong, the bus started to stop the further they got up the hill. Suddenly, the bus was about to fall off the hill but Ivy got out and saved everyone. She felt like a hero.

Aaliyah Chan (9)
Harris Primary Academy Haling Park, Croydon

THE THREE PIGS AND THE FRIENDLY WOLF

Once upon a time, there were three pigs. They went to live in the forest. The three pigs' names were Tom, Jack and Jo. To hide from the wolf they built their houses in the forest. Tom built a straw house. Jack built a wooden house and Jo built a brick house. The three pigs were afraid the wolf was going to eat them. But when the wolf came to visit he wanted to make friends. They were happy. The three pigs and the wolf played and ate together.

Aliyah Sayfoo (5)
Harris Primary Academy Haling Park, Croydon

THREE LITTLE UNICORNS

Once upon a time, there were three little unicorns walking across a river and out came a dragon breathing fire. They all ran away to their three houses. One made from straw, one from sticks and one from bricks. Two were not strong and one was strong. The straw one blew down, the stick one blew down and the brick one, it was too strong. The dragon was going to go down the chimney. They were smart, they had a boiling pot at the bottom...

Rayne Wilson-Watson (6)
Harris Primary Academy Haling Park, Croydon

BIG BAD WOLF AND THREE LITTLE PIGS

Once upon a time, there were three little pigs. The little pigs were hungry so they went to the shop to buy food but they had no money. There was a knock on the door. It was their friend, the big bad wolf. He had brought some food for the three little pigs. He said, "I saw you guys were hungry so I brought you some food to eat for lunch."
So the pigs happily took the lunch and said, "Thank you, Wolf."

Raphael Brazier (10)
Harris Primary Academy Haling Park, Croydon

CINDERELLA

A girl named Cinderella had a mum. In another country, there lived a girl named Drizella with her dad. The dad died, so Drizella went to live with Cinderella. Drizella was basically a maid, she did every chore in the house and she ate leftovers. Cinderella asked if she could go to the ball and her mum said yes. There Cinderella and the prince fell in love. One month later they got married and lived happily ever after.

Tianna Kelly (9)
Harris Primary Academy Haling Park, Croydon

BOY IN SCHOOL

One day Jack went to school and felt very shy, it was his first day. He entered his new school. Surely there were lots of pupils and teachers he could talk to. He went to class and did maths first. Break time was lonely with no friends. English was long, he wrote two pages in an hour. PE was a bit better, but history was bad. He packed for home and they lined up in order as they came out of class.

Ryan Rahman (9)
Harris Primary Academy Haling Park, Croydon

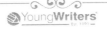

THE RAINBOW CLOUD

Once there was a cloud that felt very plain. She wanted some colour in her life. One day there came a rainbow. He looked very majestic and happy when he moved. She asked Rainbow for some colours. He said yes then they stuck together. They started to share their colour. Cloud had some colour to share with the world. Then everyone was happy forever.

Advika Yadav (6)
Harris Primary Academy Haling Park, Croydon

A MAGNIFICENT MISSION

"All systems go!" shouted the space controller, as the space rocket glided towards the launch pad. "Blast off in 10 minutes... Astronauts ready?" Excitement was building for the first mission to explore Saturn's outer rings. "They're coming now!" exclaimed the crew leader. Majestically, a figure moved towards the rocket's entrance on all fours. His big grin and white suit glistened in the sunlight. A second astronaut followed, waddling behind, wearing a black and white coat. "Strapping in... Fishy suitcases loaded... Ready for take-off!" the crew leader announced.

"Safe flight Mr Polar Bear and Mr Penguin!" The animal astronauts beamed back.

Lucy Anderson (9)
St Peter's CE Middle School, Old Windsor

THE THREE NAUGHTY GOATS GRUFF

Once there were three very naughty goats that loved mischief. Especially destroying the troll's field that once bloomed with beautiful dazzling flowers. The troll had had enough so he made a plan. When the goats were going to cross his bridge he would roar, scaring the goats away. They came to the bridge. "Let me cross!" demanded the small goat. "Not ever!" the troll replied, tossing him away.

The second goat stepped up. "Move out my way!" he cried.

Again Troll just threw him away. Before the third goat could even speak Troll quickly roared with all his might...

Elizabeth Hunt (9)
St Peter's CE Middle School, Old Windsor

CINDERELLA'S SWIMATHON

There was a girl called Cinderella. She had sisters who didn't like her. There was a swimming competition, her sisters entered. Cinderella was a swimmer but her mum wouldn't let her enter. The family went. Before they went Cinderella had snuck her swimsuit to the competition. She was up next. She swam her life out. Edward was standing there. Ella won!

"Wait!" It was Edward. "You are the best swimmer, will you come to my father's swim school? You deserve it."

"Yes, I will!"

Ella's family were upset but knew what was best for her. And so did Ella.

Harriet Bannan (10)
St Peter's CE Middle School, Old Windsor

BELLA'S DREAM

"Going out, Mum!" said Bella, opening the door and skipping down the path. Suddenly, a gust of wind blew a mysterious letter across the path. Curiously, she picked it up... It read... 'Come to the forest, follow the toadstools and meet me in my house'.
Reluctantly, she followed the instructions.
Surprised to see a wooden house, she entered with a shudder. In sight, was a beautifully iced cake.
Taking a bite, *bam!* She found herself in a cage.
Luckily, in her pocket was a hairpin, she escaped!
Sprinting home, down she fell.
"Bella, wake up!" It was all a dream.

Jessica Hyde (10)
St Peter's CE Middle School, Old Windsor

FINDING A HOME

Boom! The aliens looked on heartbroken from their spaceship as their planet exploded. Captain Bob rubbed one of his five eyes with his tentacle. Where would they go? After travelling for 100 years the aliens were running out of time, if they didn't find a planet where they could land in the next 24 hours they would run out of fuel and die. Captain Bob knew they were in trouble. How would he save his people? After frantically searching for a planet Zark yelled, "Look there!"

Suddenly Earth appeared, like a mirage. Had they finally found a home?

Sophia McEntee (9)

St Peter's CE Middle School, Old Windsor

CINDERELLA'S DISASTER

In a town called Sunny Hills, in a house, there was a family with a bright child called Cinderella. Her two sisters were named Ruby and Ashley. In the town, there was a commotion about the ball.
Six days later it was time to go. Cinderella rushed to the ball in the rain. The prince had watched Ruby for the last two hours. Cinderella burst in looking filthy. The prince came downstairs from the balcony, started dancing and asked Ruby if she would marry him. "Yes."
The prince saw Cinderella and said, "You need a wash!"
Ruby was the queen.

Ava Jarmola (10)
St Peter's CE Middle School, Old Windsor

THE BIG BAD GIRL

Once upon a time, there was a wolf called Little
Red Riding Hood (LRRH). She took her grandma
some cookies because she was unwell. She walked
in the woods to her grandma's house where she
met the big bad girl who was wicked. The big bad
girl hurried to Grandma's house because she
wanted to eat Grandma. LRRH arrived at the
house. BBG (the big bad girl) pretended to be
Grandma and wanted to hurt LRRH. LRRH asked,
"Why do you look so young?"
"It's to do with my illness," BBG replied.
LRRH then realised and ate BBG.

Lily McBride (9)
St Peter's CE Middle School, Old Windsor

MY HISTORY

A sunny morning... Warm fragrant tea and fresh pancakes are on the table. Mom just cooked. I'm dressed, it's time to go to school... But at once I hear it... A sound I've never heard in my life. It repeats again. Fear and weeping fill my chest. Mom hugs us tightly.

We have to leave the house. We travel. Days and weeks pass. A dream about meeting Dad again. Will this terrible dream end? I wake up and hear... "Daughter! You have the right to live a happy childhood." It's my dad.

The world is not without good people.

Ilona Shevchuk (9)
St Peter's CE Middle School, Old Windsor

YOU NEVER KNOW

Hundreds of years ago in the land called Festive Forest no inch was without snow. Steve, a brown-haired boy, loved nothing more than Christmas and the snowy season. Steve was strolling along with his best mate, Snotty Sizzle, when they found the biggest and oldest tree in the whole wood. The tree had stood for many centuries and stood at three giraffes tall above the ground. They had walked for quite some time when all of a sudden Snotty took his clothes off and to Steve's amazement and shock he saw Snotty Snizzle was really a devil in disguise!

Noah Richards (10)
St Peter's CE Middle School, Old Windsor

SPY CAT

Suzy sat down at the kitchen table, eating her usual burnt toast. *Ding-dong!* Suzy was shocked to open the door to a man wearing a black suit and sunglasses. He placed a large package in Suzy's hand. She closed the door and watched her mum run around, looking for her glasses. Suzy ran to her room. It was just like one of those unboxing videos she had seen. She carefully unsealed the package. She lifted the flaps. It was moving. Suzy let out a scream until reading the collar... 'Spy Cat'. What on earth could a spy cat be?

Tara Khabra (11)
St Peter's CE Middle School, Old Windsor

MARLEY AND STEVE: ORIGIN STORY

Marley was a teenager with special powers. His special powers were making portals, making stuff using his imagination and flying with his special cape. His sidekick, Steve, was a shapeshifter and they both fought crime together. Once they were fighting this guy called The Copier. He was very strong and powerful. During the fight, Steve ran away and Marley was left to fight alone. The Copier actually saw Steve using his powers to help kill Marley so Marley was left to fight both. He used his powers to kill them but they came back to life...

Harry Kirk (10)
St Peter's CE Middle School, Old Windsor

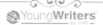

THE FIGURE

Once upon a time, there was a girl called Angela. She was a sweet girl who lived in the city. One night she was woken from her dream by rain hammering against the window. She heard footsteps on the stairs. She suddenly felt very scared. A strange shadowy figure stood in the doorway. Angela was shaking with fear and didn't know what to do. Then she heard some footsteps coming closer to her. She wanted to scream for her mum but no words came out. The figure then gave her a glass of water. It was her mum all along.

Abigail Cleaton (9)
St Peter's CE Middle School, Old Windsor

THE MYSTERY OF THE WEREWOLF

A girl, Charlotte Quinn, heard there was a new man moving in so she baked some cookies. The next day she took them to his door. She rang the doorbell but he didn't answer. So she opened the door and went upstairs. She couldn't believe her eyes. He seemed to be another creature, perhaps a werewolf. She dropped the cookies and ran. She galloped around the village shouting, "Werewolf!" but no one believed her. She needed proof!

So from that day on she wondered if anyone would ever believe her.

Beau Russell (10)

St Peter's CE Middle School, Old Windsor

THE ARCTIC WONDER

An English millionaire invented a suit that let anyone survive any climate/habitat while not needing to eat/drink for five days...

The millionaire, his wife, son and daughter went on a trip to the Arctic. As soon as they got there the parents went snow bathing so the daughter ran off and found a polar bear. It looked hungry so she gave it a fish. They became best friends. After it ate that fish they went for a swim but it got stuck under the ice. Unfortunately, it drowned the girl.

Hayden Davy (10)
St Peter's CE Middle School, Old Windsor

THE WOLF AND THE REVOLTING PIGS

"Not by the hair on my chinny chin chin!" yelled the wolf as the revolting, ugly, disgusting pigs chased after the wolf, trying to steal his hard-earned money. The wolf had just finished work building a log pile house for the snake, a treetop house for the owl and an underground house for the fox. Luckily the wolf's friend, Billy Butcher, was just around the corner and saved the wolf by making sausages and pork pies for everyone in the forest.

Freddie Blackman (9)

St Peter's CE Middle School, Old Windsor

Young Writers
Information

We hope you have enjoyed reading this book – and that you will continue to in the coming years.

If you're the parent or family member of an enthusiastic poet or story writer, do visit our website **www.youngwriters.co.uk/subscribe** and sign up to receive news, competitions, writing challenges and tips, activities and much, much more! There's lots to keep budding writers motivated!

If you would like to order further copies of this book, or any of our other titles, then please give us a call or order via your online account.

Young Writers
Remus House
Coltsfoot Drive
Peterborough
PE2 9BF
(01733) 890066
info@youngwriters.co.uk

Join in the conversation!
Tips, news, giveaways and much more!

 **YoungWritersUK** 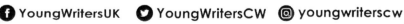 **YoungWritersCW**  **youngwriterscw**

Scan me to watch the A Twist In The Tale video!